WEB OF
THE CYCLAN

At the heart of the web glowed the mass of
Central Intelligence, the heart of the Cyclan.
Buried deep beneath miles of rock on a lonely
world, the massed brains absorbed Khai's
knowledge as a sponge sucked water. A mental
communication in the form of words, quick,
almost instantaneous:

"Dumarest? There is no possibility of doubt?"

"None."

"Your prediction as to present whereabouts?"

"Insufficient data for prediction of high
probability but certainly in the direction of the
Hichen Cloud."

That was all. The rest was sheer
intoxication . . . Always it was the same. One
day Khai would be a part of it. His brain,
removed, would join the others, hooked in a
unified whole, all working to a common end:

The complete and absolute control of the
entire galaxy. The elimination of waste and the
direction of effort so that every man and every
world would become the parts of a universal
machine.

D0720388

JACK
OF
SWORDS

E. C. Tubb

DAW BOOKS, INC.

DONALD A. WOLLHEIM, PUBLISHER

1301 Avenue of the Americas
New York, N. Y.   10019

DEDICATION

To John Newman

FIRST PRINTING, JUNE 1976

1 2 3 4 5 6 7 8 9

PRINTED IN U.S.A.

JACK
OF
SWORDS

Chapter 1

At sunset the sky of Teralde was painted with vibrant swaths of brilliant color; minute crystals of air-borne dust refracting the light so that the entire bowl of the firmament looked as if some cosmic artist had spilled his palette in a profusion of inspired genius. An eye-catching spectacle but one which, for Dumarest, had long ceased to hold charm.

He walked through the streets gilded with dying light, past tall houses fashioned of stone, the windows small, the doors thick and tightly barred. Even the shops were like small fortresses, their wares jealously guarded, reluctantly displayed. The field, as usual, was empty, the barren dirt devoid of the weight of a single vessel. The gate set into the perimeter fence was unmanned, a sure sign that no ship was expected.

"Nothing." The agent, a Hausi, leaned back in his chair. His ebony face, scarred with the caste marks of his guild, was bland. "Ships will arrive eventually, of course, but Teralde is not a commercial world. Only when the beasts have been processed and shipments are available will the traders come. Until then all we can hope for is some tourists."

Luxury vessels carrying jaded dilettantes, the rich and curious with money to burn and time to waste. But Dumarest had no time—unless a ship arrived soon he would be stranded.

He said, "I need work."

"Work?" The Hausi shrugged. "My friend, on Teralde the desire is not enough. You need to own special skills. Your profession?"

"I can do most things which need to be done."

"Of course. Do I reveal doubt?" Yethan Ctonat selected a comfit from an ornamented box and crushed the candied morsel between strong teeth. "But, you understand, I represent my guild. To place a man who cannot perform the

1

skills he claims to own would reflect on my reputation. And demand is small. Are you a master of genetic manipulation? A physician? A veterinarian? I tell you frankly, we have no need of gamblers."

"Do I look a gambler?"

"A man who travels is always that," said the agent smoothly. "To drift from world to world, never certain of what he will find, what else can such a man be? Especially if he travels Low. The fifteen-percent death rate is a risk none but a gambler would take. And you have traveled Low, have you not?"

"To often, riding doped, frozen, and ninety percent dead in caskets designed for the transportation of animals. Cheap travel—all that could be said for it.

"I will not deceive you," said Yethan Ctonat. "As you must have discovered, there is no hope of normal employment on this world. You work for the Owners or for those they tolerate or you do not work at all. And for every vacancy there is a host of applicants." He added, casually, "For a man like you there is only one way to survive on Teralde."

Dumarest was curt. "To fight?"

"You have guessed it. Blood has a universal appeal. If you are interested—" The agent broke off, reaching for another comfit. "It's all I can offer."

And all Dumarest had expected, but the attempt had had to be made. The colors in the sky were fading as he walked through the city and toward the wilderness at the edge of which sprawled the slums. Lowtowns were always the same and in his time he had seen too many of them. Sometimes they were huddles of shacks, tents, and shelters crudely fashioned from whatever materials were at hand; at others as on Teralde, they were simple boxes built of stone and set in neat array. But shacks or buildings the atmosphere was identical.

A miasma compounded of despair and poverty, the reek of a world which held no pride, no hope, nothing but the bleak concentration of the moment, the need to survive yet one more day, one more hour. The refuge of those without work or money. Had they been slaves they would have been fed and clothed, a responsibility to their owners. As it was they formed a pool of cheap labor which cost nothing, the only expense being the warren in which they lived and bred and died.

"Earl!" A man came running toward Dumarest as he entered one of the buildings. "Earl, have you decided?"

Cran Elem was small, thin, his cheeks sunken, the bones prominent. Beneath the rags he wore his wasted flesh and bone gave him the fragility of a child.

Dumarest made no answer, climbing the stairs to the flat roof there to stand and look at the sky. Dusk was thickening and would soon yield to night, the darkness heralded by the glitter of early stars.

Stars like the eyes he had seen too often in the shadows surrounding a ring. The avid, hungry eyes of those eager for the sight of blood and pain. Their coldness was the chill of naked steel, their gleam that of razored edge and point. To fight, to kill and maim, to win the price of a meal so as to live to fight again. He had done it before and would again if all else failed, but there could be a better way.

To Cran he said, "Assemble and warn the men. We leave in an hour."

The storm broke at midnight with a sudden flurry of lightning followed by thunder and a driving rain. Crouched beneath the fronds of stunted vegetation Dumarest felt its impact on his head, the deluge filling his mouth and nostrils so that he had to bend his face in order to breathe. On all sides the gritty soil turned into an oozing, alluvial mud.

"Earl!" From the darkness Cran edged close, his voice strained, echoing his despair. "Earl! It's a bust!"

"Wait!"

"It's useless. We tried but this is hopeless. We'd best get back to town."

A flash illuminated him, thunder crashing as Dumarest reached out and caught an arm. Beneath his fingers he could feel the stringy muscle, the stick of bone. In his grip the man was helpless.

"Wait," he said again. "This storm could help us."

"Help?" Cran almost sobbed in his disappointment. "With mud up to our ankles and rain in our eyes? The storm will have unsettled the beasts and they're bad enough at the best of times." His voice rose to the edge of hysteria. "I thought we'd have a chance but the luck is against us. Damn the luck. Damn it all to hell!"

He cried out as Dumarest's hand slapped his cheek.

"Earl!"

"Control yourself." Dumarest freed the arm. "Get the others."

"You're going back?"

"Just do as I say."

They came like ghosts, revealed in stark detail by the intermittent flashes, the dirt which had stained faces and hands gone now, washed away by the rain. Like Cran they wore rags, torn and discarded garments salvaged from garbage, broken shoes and naked feet wrapped in layers of rotting cloth. Their hair, plastered close, accentuated their skull-like appearance. Starving men who would be dead soon unless they obtained food.

Among them Dumarest looked solid, reassuring, his clothing scuffed but whole, the gray plastic of tunic, pants and boots gleaming with a wet slickness.

He said, "Cran, how far to the compound?"

"A mile, maybe less, but—"

"This storm will help us. The guards will remain in shelter and the lightning will be blamed for anything affecting the electronic system. The animals will be together and easy to take. Before dawn you'll all have bellies full of meat."

"Or be dead," said a man bleakly.

"Today, tomorrow, what's the difference?" said another. "I'm willing to take a chance if Earl will lead us."

"I'll lead you," said Dumarest. "And there'll be no quitting. If any man tries to leave I'll cut him down. Understand?" He paused as thunder rolled and, as it faded, said, "We've no choice and the storm will make it easy. Just keep down and merge with the ground. Freeze if a light shines your way. Work as a unit and we can't go wrong."

Words to stiffen their resolve, but a man had a question.

"When we reach the compound who goes in?"

"I will," said Dumarest. "Ready? Let's get on with it."

Cran led the way and Dumarest followed him close as they left the poor shelter. It was too early to move—later the rain would ease a little, but waiting would rob the others of enthusiasm. What had to be done must be done fast and they had to be gone long before dawn.

A blur of light and the compound came into sight. The rain lashed against the mesh of the high fence and the lights ringing it, spraying and misting the installation so as to give it the insubstantial quality of a dream. A dream shattered by the sudden, snarling roar of a beast as it slammed itself against the fence.

From a tower a searchlight threw a cone of brilliance, the beam tracing a path over milling shapes, settling on the fence, dying as, satisfied, the guard killed the illumination.

Without hesitation Dumarest led the way to within feet of the mesh well away from the tower. At his orders men vanished like ghosts into the rain to take up positions at either side. At intervals they would jar the mesh to create a distraction.

"Cran!"

From within his clothing the man produced wire and a set of cutters. Quickly he hooked up a jumper-circuit, and resting the cutters on the mesh, glanced at Dumarest.

"Now?"

"Wait until the next flash."

It came with a livid coruscation, closer than before, dirt pluming as electronic energy tore at the ground. As thunder rolled the mesh parted in a narrow slit through which Dumarest thrust himself. Speed now was all-important and as the searchlight stabbed to one side where a man had jarred the fence he dived toward the nearest animal.

It was as large as a horse, horned, the hooves like razors, the tail ending in a club of bone. A chelach, its eyes small, set deep in ringed projections of bone; the mouth, open, showed teeth as sharp as chisels. A beast disturbed by the storm and bristling with anger. For a second it watched and then, as Dumarest moved closer, it charged.

Its size belied its speed. An engine of bone and muscle weighing half a ton, it jerked from a standstill to the speed of a running man in a numbing explosion of energy. Fast as it was Dumarest was faster. He sprang aside, his arm lifting as it drew level, the knife he had lifted from his boot rising, stabbing, the edge slicing at the arteries of the throat as he dragged it clear.

Blood fountained to splash on the ground, his body; carmine smears washed away by the rain but leaving its sickly scent to hang on the air. As the beast halted close to the fence he struck again, the point driving deep between the ribs, the hilt jarring against the hide as the blade dug into the heart.

"Earl!" Cran stared, incredulous. "How—I've never seen a man move as fast."

"The rope. Quick!"

It came toward him like a snake, a thing of carefully woven strands of salvaged wire. Looping it over the head Dumarest ran back toward the fence and, with the aid of others, hauled the carcass toward the gap. The rain helped as he had known it would, the mud acting like an oil. He snarled with impatience as the animal jammed, and setting his feet deep in the slime, threw the strength of back and shoulders against the wire. It grew taut, hummed like a plucked string, stretched a little but held. With a sudden rush the mass passed through the opening and within seconds was clear.

"Keep pulling," snapped Dumarest. "Hurry!"

They needed no urging, panting as they struggled against the weight, freezing as the beam of the searchlight swept toward them. It touched the upper part of the torn fence, hesitated, then turned away as one of the men, recognizing the danger, jarred the mesh.

Their luck was holding—but time was running out.

Dumarest strained, edged to the right, and found the hollow he had noted earlier. A final heave and the dead animal rolled down the slope to come to rest in a pool of watery mud.

"Get the others, Cran. Be careful."

As the man slipped away Dumarest set to work, his knife plunging, ripping, blood flying as he flensed and dismembered the carcass. Those watching snatched fragments of meat, gulping them like dogs, licking the blood from their hands with a feral hunger.

"Here!" Dumarest handed out hunks of dripping meat. "Don't take more than you can easily carry. Leave as soon as you're loaded. Wait for the next flash and freeze when the next one follows."

"The liver," said a man. "Don't forget the liver."

"We'll share it on the way and eat as we go. Cran?"

Like an eel he slipped into the hollow with his companions.

"Hurry," he panted. "The guards are suspicious and they could have spotted the torn fence. If so they'll be coming to investigate."

Men with guns and portable searchlights who would not hesitate to shoot.

"Keep watch," ordered Dumarest. "Let me know if they come this way. The rest of you, get moving. Move, damn you! Move!"

Minutes later he followed, wiping his knife and thrusting it into his boot before lifting his load. Together they vanished into the darkness, shielded by the storm, invisible to the guards who finally came to investigate. They found the cut fence, but rain had washed away the blood and filled the traces with oozing mud. It wasn't until the dawn they made count and found the discarded bones, head, hooves, tail, and intestines of the slaughtered beast.

Chapter 2

Pacula had set the table, decorating it with fine glass and delicate flowers set in vases of crystal, little touches he could have done without but which impressed the Owners who came to visit. Kel Accaus was openly envious and paid unmistakable court to the woman, clumsy in his flattery.

"Pacula, my dear, your brother should be proud of you. Had I someone like yourself to act as my hostess I should not spend as much time as I do in the field. Tien, your health."

A toast which Tien Harada acknowledged with a bare inclination of the head. He had no great love for Accaus but had invited the man from necessity. Only a fool made an enemy of a man whose lands joined one's own, and yet the way he looked at Pacula would, in other times, have been grounds for a quarrel.

"You are kind, Kel," she said. "But surely you should reserve your compliments for someone younger than I?"

"What has youth to do with beauty?" he demanded. "In you I see the epitome of womanhood. If I were a poet I would compose a work in your honor. As it is, I can only state a simple truth in simple words. Your loveliness puts our sunsets to shame. You agree, Chan?"

"How can I deny it?" Chan Catiua bowed, gracious in his gesture. "Tien, a most pleasant meal."

A comment echoed by the others present and, Tien recognized, a neat way to turn the conversation. Politic too, while beautiful in her way, Pacula was no longer young and the excessive flattery could hold a tinge of mockery. Not that Accaus was capable of such subtlety, but a man couldn't be too careful and shame, once given, could never be erased.

Now, as the servants cleared the table and set out flagons of wine and bowls of succulent fruits, Tien Harada looked at his guests. Owners all, aside from one, and he was of no account. Pacula's whim and one he had tolerated—if the man could bring her ease, what right had he to complain? Yet sitting as he did, barely touching the food, a bleak contrast in his brown, homespun robe, the monk looked more like a skeleton at the feast than a privileged guest. Some wine would warm him, perhaps, and Tien gestured for a servant to fill his glass.

"Thank you, no." Brother Vray rested his hand on the container.

"You refuse my hospitality, Brother?"

"That, never, but a sufficiency is enough. And I have work awaiting me."

"The consolation of the poor," sneered Accaus. "A pat on the head for the unfortunate and a scrap of concentrate to ease their labors. No man should eat unless he works for what he puts into his mouth."

"And if no work is offered, brother?" The monk's voice was gentle as were his eyes. An old voice, the eyes in a face seamed and creased with years and deprivation. "You would be more commiserate if you were to remember that, but for the grace of God, you would be one of their number. Charity, brother, is a virtue."

"Professed by many but practiced by few," said Catiua dryly. "And your charity has an edge, Monk, is that not so? Before receiving your Bread of Forgiveness a suppliant kneels beneath the Benediction Light and is instilled with the command never to kill. Am I right?"

"You are entitled to your opinion, my lord."

"Am I right?"

"And, if you are, what is the harm?" Pacula was quick to come to his defense, for which Vray was grateful. Chan Catiua could be guessing, but he had stumbled on the truth. "Can it be wrong to prevent a man from taking the life of another?"

"No," boomed Kel and then, with sly maliciousness, added, "A pity the restriction didn't apply to beasts, eh, Tien?"

Trust the fool for having mentioned it, and Tien felt again the anger he had experienced when staring at the remains of the slaughtered animal. A rage so intense that it seemed impossible that whoever was responsible, no matter where they might be, could not have been blasted by the naked ferocity of his hatred. His prize bull slaughtered, a fortune lost, and himself held to ridicule. The guards—he felt the muscles jerk in his face as he thought about them. Useless fools who had

been asleep, careless, stupid, well, at least they had paid.
Black-listed, they would be lucky to get any job at all. To
hell with them. Let them starve together with their families.
His bull had been worth a hundred such scum.

Casually, Catiua turned the knife. "Days now, Tien, and
still no word of the culprits?"

"None." Tien's hand trembled as he poured himself wine.
"But I will find them. They will pay."

"According to the law?"

"Yes." Tien met the other's eyes, cool, slightly amused.
"They will pay," he said grimly. "No matter who they might
be or how high. This I swear!"

"You think an Owner might be responsible?" A man spoke
sharply from where he sat at the table. "Do you, Tien
Harada?"

"The possibility has not escaped me, Yafe Zoppius." Tien
was coldly formal. "It is being investigated."

"If Ibius Avorot's men came snooping around my land
they will get short measure. That I promise. You forget yourself in your suspicions, Tien." His tone softened a little.
"That I can understand. It was a grievous loss. A prime
specimen of genetic manipulation which would have bred a
new and stronger line. But you must not accuse your
friends."

Friends on the surface, competitors beneath, each jealous
of the other's prosperity. Yet the facade had to be
maintained, unity shown, and a common face presented to
the outside. The monk, for example—he could learn more
than he should. The Universal Church had friends in high
places, and who could tell what gossip they carried? It had
been a mistake to permit his presence. Pacula, at times, went
too far.

Later, when the assembly had departed, he spoke to her
about it.

"The monk, sister—is it wise to advertise your friendship?"

"I look to him for help."

"Which will be given at a price, naturally. More money
wasted on a futile quest. The girl is dead—can't you accept
that? Culpea is dead."

"No!" He saw the sudden pallor of her face, the lines suddenly appearing and betraying her age, so that, for a moment, she looked haggard. Then, with an effort, she con-

trolled herself, old defenses coming to the rescue. "You musn't say that, Tien. There is no proof. No—" she swallowed and forced herself to continue. "No body was ever found."

"The raft crashed. Her nurse was discovered in a crevass. The guards were scattered and none alive to tell what happened. But we can guess. Please, sister, accept the facts. It is better so."

"She could have been found," she insisted. "Taken by some passing wanderer. Such things happen. I must continue the search, Tien. I must!"

Years now and still she hoped and yet he hadn't the heart to be ruthless. Even so, there had to be an end to the money she squandered.

"You have tried the monks before," he reminded. "Your donations were more than generous, but to no avail. Money is scarce, and with the bull dead, economies have to be made. I am sorry, Pacula, but my patience is exhausted. Search on if you must, but don't look to me for further help."

"You deny me my right?"

"You have had that and more. There must be an end." Pausing, he added more gently, "One thing more I will do. On Heidah are skilled physicians who can eliminate hurtful memories and replace them with comforting illusions. Go to them, Pacula, have them eradicate this torment. Forget the child and gain a measure of peace."

"And you will pay for it?"

Relief at her acquiescence made him overlook the calculation in her eyes. "Of course. Tell me how much and it will be yours. You have my word."

"Which has never been broken." Her smile was a mask. "I will consider it, Tien."

He did not see the hand she held at her side, the fingers clenched, the knuckles taut beneath the skin. Nor did he observe the muscles tense beneath the smile which accentuated the line of her jaw. To him her words were enough.

"Have an early night," he urged. "You have been upset since the storm. And with reason," he added quickly. "That I do not deny. But you are fatigued. A good sleep and you will feel better."

She said flatly, "Thank you, Tien, I will follow your advice. But later. Tonight I have promised to visit Sufan Noyoka."

"That dreamer?" Tien made no effort to hide his contempt. "The man is mad."

"But harmless."

"Can madness ever be that?" He shrugged, expecting no answer and receiving none. "Well, do as you wish, but be careful. You promise?"

"I promise."

He left her at that, satisfied, his mind busy with other things. The pain of his recent loss was a nagging ache which left little concern for the rightness of a decision made. Let her visit Noyoka. Perhaps, in each other's company, they could find a common ease. Madness had an affinity to madness and, reluctant as he was to admit it, his sister was far from sane.

When a boy, Ibius Avorot had seen a man flayed and staked out in the sun as a punishment for the unlawful killing of a beast. His father had been at pains to point out the necessity for such harsh treatment, his hand gripping the thin shoulder, pain emphasizing the lesson.

An animal killed, in itself nothing if it had not been for the value, but what next? Once allow a threat against the established order and there would be no end. Shops raided, men killed, a mass of starving wretches bursting from their confines and demanding food as a right instead of a reward. Give it to them and where would be the power held by the Owners? To be charitable was to invite destruction. To survive on Teralde a man had to be strong.

Logic which had confounded the boy as he was forced to watch the man die. Surely a man was of greater value than a beast? And if hunger turned men savage, then why not feed them and eliminate the danger? Concepts which his father had done his best to beat from his son and, when learning, Ibius had confessed his errors, had been satisfied.

A hard man who had died as he lived, one respected by the Owners, who had not hesitated to elect his son to the vacated position. And the years had brought a cynical contempt for those who begged for the food they could have taken by right. That lesson at least he had learned, only the strong could survive—but never again did he want to see a screaming creature wearing the shape of a man die in such a fashion.

And yet, it seemed, soon he would have no choice.

"Commissioner?" Usan Labria had entered his office and plumped herself down without invitation. Old, raddled, the gems on her fingers accentuating the sere and withered flesh. Paint made her face a grotesque mask in which her eyes, cold, shrewd, gleamed like splintered glass.

"My lady, this is an honor."

"An inconvenience, Commissioner. For once be honest."

Once, perhaps, he would have accepted the invitation, now he was not so foolish. "The visit of an Owner could never be that, my lady. You have a problem?"

"We all have a problem. This bull of Harada's—when are you going to find who killed it?"

"Your interest?"

"Don't be a fool, man." Her voice, like her face, was a distortion of what a woman's should be. Harsh, rough, strained as if with pain. "Harada suspects an Owner is responsible. Unless the culprits are found he will be tempted to take action and the last thing we want is an internecine war. The last time it happened a third of the breeding stock was destroyed and two Owners assassinated. That was before your time, but I remember it. I don't want it to happen again."

"It won't, my lady."

"Which means that you've discovered something." Her eyes narrowed a trifle. "Why haven't you made an arrest? How much longer will you keep us all in suspense? I insist you take action, Commissioner, and fast. If not, another will take your place."

Another threat to add to the rest, but he could understand her concern. Her lands were arid, her herd small, a war could wipe her out and end her power. For such a woman that was unthinkable.

He said quietly, "To take action isn't enough. There is the question of proof."

"Surely that can be found?" She edged closer to the desk, her voice lowered. "Who was it? Eldaret? Jelkin? Repana? Who?"

Owners all, and her suspicions were proof of how they regarded each other. The bull, used, would have put them all at a disadvantage.

She frowned at his answer. "Not an Owner! Man, do you realize what you are saying? It would have taken a rifle to kill that beast, a laser even. Men would have needed a raft and lights to spot the target. Who but an Owner could have arranged it?"

"Think of the facts, my lady."

"I know them." She was curt. "A beast killed and butchered—obviously done to avoid suspicion. The fence cut and the animal removed so as to hide the real objective. Have you questioned the guards?"

"I know my business, my lady."

She ignored the reproof. "They must have been bribed. Question them again and this time be less gentle. It is something you should have done before."

"And will the ravings and accusations of a man in torment provide satisfactory evidence?" With an effort he mastered himself. Never could he afford the luxury of betraying his true feelings. "The problem must be solved to the satisfaction of Tien Harada. Unless it is, his suspicions will remain as will the possibility of reprisal. I—" He broke off as his phone hummed its signal. To the face on the screen he snapped, "What is it?"

"A report from Officer Harm, sir. A man was reported for trying to sell meat."

"Sun-dried?"

"Yes."

"And?" Avorot's voice reflected his impatience. "Speak up, man."

"He was suspicious and tried to run. Officer Harm had to shoot. The man is now in hospital."

"Dead?"

"Wounded, but critical. I thought it best—"

The screen died as Avorot broke the connection. To the woman he said, "My apologies, my lady, but this is urgent. I must speak to that man before he dies."

He lay on a cot in a room painted green and brown, the colors of earth and growth, but one hue was missing, the scarlet of blood. Avorot looked at the thin face, then at the doctor hovering close.

"Can he talk?"

"He is in terminal coma."

"That isn't answering my question. Can you give him drugs in order to make him speak?"

"He's dying, Commissioner. Your officer aimed too well,

the bullet severed the spine and lacerated the lungs. The loss of blood was intense and that, coupled with shock—"

"I am not interested in your diagnosis," snapped Avorot. "Nor in your implied criticism of my officer. The man is a criminal who refused to obey an order. He holds information I must have. It is your responsibility to see that I get it. Call me when the man can speak."

Outside the room Officer Harm was waiting. A big, beefy man with little imagination who stared unflinchingly at his superior.

"What happened?" demanded Avorot. "Go into detail."

"I was on patrol close to the field, as you'd instructed, Commissioner. The news that a ship is expected had got around and there was the usual crowd waiting for it to land. Scum, mostly, those with nothing else to do. You know how it is."

"Go on."

"Gilus Scheem sent me word by a man working for him. Someone was trying to sell him unlicensed meat. He was gone when I arrived but I had his description and managed to spot him. I yelled at him to halt but he just kept going. So I shot him."

And the fool had aimed to kill. A bullet in the air would have been enough, or a chase to run the man down, but Harm wouldn't have thought of that.

"And the meat?"

"Here, sir. I thought you'd want to see it."

In that, at least, he'd shown sense. Avorot took the package and ripped it open to reveal the strips of tissue inside. He rubbed his fingers over a piece and held them to his nostrils. No scent of smoke, but that was expected. The sun itself would have been good enough for a man who knew what he was doing. His tongue told him more; no spice, nothing but the flesh itself. No commercial house would have turned out such a product.

"Let me taste that." Usan Labria had insisted on accompanying him. She grunted as she handed back the package. "Not stolen from a warehouse, that's for sure, nor from a shop. And no processing plant would turn out such rubbish. What is it, Commissioner?"

"Owner Harada's bull."

"What?" She was incredulous. "Are you telling me that animal was slaughtered simply for its meat? That men came in the storm and killed it and—no!" Firmly she shook her head. "It's impossible. It couldn't be done."

For answer he held out the package.

"Meat," she admitted. "Unlicensed and poorly cured, but still not proof that it came from Harada's bull."

"From where, then? The slaughterhouses?" Avorot shook his head. "Every ounce is accounted for. I'll admit that there could be some leakage from culled beasts and at times the sporting hunters grow careless. But this is the wrong time of year for that. This meat has been recently cured. It is proof which could clear the Owners from blame."

And lead him to those responsible if the dying man could talk. Back in the room Avorot stared down at him, at the pale face, blank now like a waxen mask, the eyes closed, only the slight lifting of his chest telling that he was still alive.

"I've given him what I can," said the doctor quietly. "I guarantee nothing, but there could be a moment before he dies when he might regain consciousness. You can talk to him then, but you will have to be quick."

"Any history?"

"None. My guess is he is a stranded traveler—we have a lot of those living in the Warren. His hands are abraded and his clothes were rags. I'd say he's been living in the wilderness for days at least." The doctor reached out and touched the flaccid throat. "A fool," he said dispassionately. "He should have eaten the meat, not tried to sell it."

A medical judgment, but the man had wanted more than a full stomach. The meat would have fetched money, had the dealer been less scrupulous—not much but enough for a stake at a gaming table and the chance to build it into enough for a Low passage. A journey which would have killed him, but a desperate man would have been willing to take the chance.

On the cot he stirred a little, a bubble of froth rising between his lips to break, to leave a ruby smear.

"Listen to me." Avorot leaned close. "Who was with you when you killed the bull? Who?"

"A ship ... coming ... a chance ..." The words were faint, the rustle of dry leaves blown by the wind. "Move now before—God, the pain! The pain!"

"It will pass. Talk now and I'll order you the best treatment available. Who arranged it? Who led you?"

The lips parted to emit a thin stream of blood which traced

a path over the pale cheek and stained the pillow. The eyes, open, grew suddenly clear, the moment of full consciousness the doctor had promised might occur.

Quickly Avorot said, "I can help you, but you must help me. Who led you on your trip to kill the animal? What is his name?"

"Help me?"

"The best of care. Food. Money for a High passage. I swear it. But the name. You must give me the name."

"I'm dying!" The man stared with glazing eyes. "Earl warned me, but I wouldn't listen. I was a fool."

"Earl?"

"Dumarest."

"What about him?"

"Fast!" The voice was slurring as the man slipped toward death. "The fastest thing I ever saw. Killed the beast with a knife. Cut its throat and drove steel into its heart. Earl, I . . ."

"Who else?" Avorot was sharp. "Who else was with you?"

It was too late, the man was dead, but he had heard enough. Avorot closed the staring eyes and straightened, conscious of the acrid odor of the woman, the stench of sickness.

"You heard?"

"A name," she admitted. "And an attribute."

It was enough. When the ship landed he would have the man.

Chapter 3

It was a small vessel carrying a score of sightseers. They disembarked at noon and would stay a few days, watching the sunsets and hunting selected beasts, returning with trophies of ears and tails, later to leave.

Dumarest watched them from the edge of the field, staying clear of the crowd, conscious of the attention the guards were paying to those pressing close. Only when the crew made an appearance did he move toward the gate.

Casually he fell into step behind a uniformed figure following the man into a tavern. He was big, with a hard, craggy face. He looked up in annoyance as Dumarest dropped into the seat at his side.

"Save your breath, the answer's no."

"The answer to what?"

"You asking for a free drink. You want charity, go to the monks."

"You move too fast, friend," said Dumarest mildly. "All I want is to talk. You the handler?"

"Yes."

"Where are you headed next?"

"Ephrine and then back to Homedale. I won't be sorry to get there." He glanced at the girl who had come to take his order, then at Dumarest. "You buying?"

"I'm buying." As the girl set down the goblets and took the money Dumarest said, "A bad trip?"

"I've had better. The ship was chartered to the Manager of Ralech—that's on Homedale and he wants nothing but the best. Tourists are fine when it comes to tips but this bunch is something special. Complaints all the time and the stewards are run ragged trying to please them. You a traveler?"

"Yes."

"I thought so, you can always tell. And I'm betting you want passage, right?"

"Can it be arranged?"

"No." The man sipped at his wine. "I'm giving it to you straight. The caskets are full of trophies and other junk and we've no room for anyone traveling Low. Sorry, but there it is."

"How about a berth? I've worked on ships and can handle the job. A table too if I have to."

"We've got a gambler and he's good. You've money?" He emptied his goblet as Dumarest nodded. "Enough for a Low passage, right? Well, it's just possible I might be able to fix something. You any good with a knife?"

"I can fight if I have to."

"Some of the young sports have a yen for combat. On Homedale a few scars win a man respect and they like to think they're good. You'll have to use a practice blade, of course, and make sure you don't get yourself killed, but that's up to you. If you're good you can handle it. With luck you could win a little money as prizes and there's always the chance of tips. Some of the women could take a fancy to you." He looked at Dumarest's face. "In fact, I'd bet on it. Interested?"

"Yes."

The handler looked at his empty goblet and smiled as Dumarest ordered it to be refilled.

"We could get along. Tell you what, I'll speak to the Old Man. If he agrees I'll let you know. Be at the gate an hour before sunset."

A chance and he had to take it. As the sun lowered and the first traces of vibrant color began to tinge the sky Dumarest walked toward the field. The guards, he noticed, were behind the fence and the gate was closed. Before it stood a cluster of others, men who could have no hope of gaining a passage but who had been drawn by a hopeless longing. Cran Elem was among them.

"Earl!" He came forward, smiling. "Do you think we've got a chance?"

"At what?"

"A passage, what else? They need stewards, no pay but a chance to get away from here. The officer—" He broke off, frowning at Dumarest's expression. "Something wrong?"

"Who did you talk to?"

"The second engineer. He came out with the passengers. I took a chance and spoke to him."

"And he told you to be here an hour before sunset?"

"Yes." Cran was defensive. "I know you told us to stay hidden, but Aret came to town and I followed him. It's all right," he added. "A begger told me what happened. He was shot by a guard."

"Killed?"

"He was dead when they took him to hospital. He didn't talk, Earl. He couldn't."

Or so the man believed. He wanted to believe as he wanted to hope in the chance of a passage, but on this ship, without money, that was impossible. Then why had the officer told him to be at the gate? Him and, perhaps, the others?

Dumarest remembered the handler, the man had seemed honest enough, but so would any actor playing a part. If he had lied—Dumarest's face tightened at the thought of it, but there would be time later for revenge. Now he sensed the closing jaws of a trap.

"Get away from here, Cran. Fast."

"Why?" Suspicion darkened the thin face. "You want to cut down the competition? Earl, I didn't think—"

"Shut up and move! I'm coming with you!"

There were more ways than one of getting on a field and, under cover of darkness, the fence could be scaled and the handler faced. Now he had to obey his instincts, the in-grained caution which had saved him so often before.

Casually he edged from the gate, his eyes searching the area. Men stood in casual attitudes in a wide semicircle all around, leaning on walls, apparently killing time, some talking, all dressed in civilian clothing. To one side a group were having trouble with a chelach, a bull, scraggy, the hide scarred, the tip of one horn broken. It snarled as it was driven with electronic probes, an animal being taken to slaughter—but why was it being driven toward the gate?

The trap closed before he had taken three strides.

Snarling, the animal reared, stung by electronic whips, goaded beyond the endurance of its savage temper. Turning, it was stung again, back hurting still more, only by running could it escape its tormentors. And before it rested the gate and the cluster of men.

They scattered as it came, some desperately trying to climb the fence, falling back from the mesh, which gave no hold for hands and feet. Dumarest dodged, feeling the blow of a horn, the plastic of his tunic slit as by a knife, only the metal

mesh embedded with the material saving him from injury.
Rolling where he fell he sprang to his feet, seeing Cran running, to be caught, gored, tossed high, to fall with his intestines trailing from his ripped stomach, dead before he hit the
ground.

Barely pausing, the bull reared, pawed the ground, and
then, like a storm, came directly toward him.

Again he dodged, the knife in his hand darting to draw
blood from the scarred hide. A blow meant to hurt, not to
kill, to sting and not to maim. He backed, moving away from
the gate, the helpless men crouched, watchful.

The eyes were too well protected, the head solid bone. He
could slash the throat, but there was no storm to confuse the
beast, and too many were watching. The snout, he decided.
The muzzle would be tender. Stab it and the beast would
flinch. Continue and it would turn and head toward the town.

Like a dancer he faced it, the knife glittering in his hand,
darting, withdrawing as he sprang aside from the horns, the
tip now stained with blood, more smearing the muzzle, the
lips drawn back from the gleaming teeth.

Again, a third time, then he heard the crack of shots, bullets slamming into the beast from the guns of uniformed
guards.

Guns which leveled on his body as the animal fell.

"You betrayed yourself," said Ibius Avorot. "I want you to
understand that. I also want you to understand that I am in
no doubt that you killed the bull belonging to Owner Harada.
It would simplify matters if you were to confess."

Dumarest said nothing, looking at the room to which he
had been taken. It was bleak, relieved only by a bowl of
flowers, a gentle touch at varience with the stark furnishings,
the desk, the men who sat facing him. A man still young but
with touches of premature gray showing at his temples. His
uniform of ocher and green.

He was not alone. To one side sat a couple, the man older
than the woman, Tien Harada and his sister Pacula. At the
other sat Usan Labria, who had insisted attending the interrogation as an impartial observer. A demand Avorot could not
refuse and to which Harada had been forced to agree. There
must be no later suspicion of manipulated evidence—the matter was too important for that.

As the silence lengthened Avorot said, "Your name is Earl

Dumarest. You arrived on Teralde on the trader *Corade*. From where?"

"Laconde."

"And before that?"

"Many worlds," said Dumarest. "I am a traveler."

"A drifter," snapped Tien Harada. "Useless scum causing trouble."

An interruption Averot could have done without. He said firmly, "With respect, Owner Harada, I am conducting this investigation. You are interested, I am sure, in determining the truth."

"The truth," said Harada and added pointedly, "Not your interpretation of it. I am fully aware that it would be most convenient if it was decided an outsider killed my bull."

An implied insult which Avorot chose to ignore. Glancing at the folder lying open before him on the desk he said to Dumarest, "Your planet of origin?"

"Earth."

"Earth?" Averot looked up. "An odd name for a world. I have never heard of it. But no matter. You understand why you are here and the charge made against you? It is that, on the night of the storm, you conspired with others to unlawfully slaughter a beast belonging to Owner Harada. The penalty for that is death."

Dumarest said flatly, "If I am guilty."

"Of course."

"And isn't there a matter of proof?"

"Naturally. Teralde is not a barbaric world and we observe the law. But there is proof. A confession was made before witnesses." Avorot glanced at Usan Labria. "You were named and implicated. Some meat was recovered and the contents of the stomach of the man killed before the gate contained more. He was your associate."

"Was," said Dumarest bitterly. "Did he have to die?"

"That was unfortunate, but it was essential to prove a point. Owner Harada found it hard to believe that a man could kill a chelach with only a knife. You showed him that it could be done."

And had shown his speed, the thing the dying man had mentioned, the incredibly fast reflexes which alone made such a thing possible. Leaning back, Avorot looked at the man before him. A hard man, he decided, one long accustomed to making his own way. Such a man would not willingly have starved.

Pacula said, "Commissioner, what you say is impressive, but surely there is doubt? The witness could have lied. What makes you so certain this is the man?"

"Because he fits the pattern, my lady."

"Pattern?"

"When the crime was reported I was faced with a choice of alternatives," Avorot explained. "An Owner could have been responsible for reasons we all know, but I could find no evidence against any of them. The alternative was that the animal had been killed solely for its meat. In that case a man of a special type had to be responsible. Consider what needed to be done. Men assembled, for he would have needed at least a guide and others to create a distraction. The fence cut, the beast killed and butchered, the meat transported to the wilderness later to be dried in the sun."

"For what reason?"

"Food, my lady." Avorot masked his irritation. Why couldn't they see what to him was clear?

"But this man has money. He had no reason to steal."

Again she had missed the point and he took a pleasure in explaining how he had arrived at what could only be the true answer.

To Dumarest he said, "You are a clever man, shrewd and with courage, but you were unlucky. Those who deal with others always run the risk of betrayal, but it was one you had to take. Let us review the situation. You landed on Teralde with the price of a Low passage and within a matter of hours you discovered that work was unobtainable. Some men would have gambled and hoped to win, others would have used their money to buy food, but you know better than to do either. Without money you would be stranded and a man who is desperate to win never does. What remained? How to survive with your money intact so as to buy a passage to another world? And how to build up your strength so as to survive a Low passage?"

Pacula said, "Commissioner?"

"A man needs to be strong to ride in a casket, my lady," said Avorot, not looking at her. "He needs fat on which to sustain his metabolism. Chelach meat is the most concentrated form of natural nourishment we know. A half pound can provide energy for a day. The dead beast provided enough to maintain a dozen men for weeks. You took a chance, Dumarest, but a good one. Simply to stay out of sight and save your money for when a ship came. To make those who had worked with you do the same. For you that would not have been difficult. The threat of your knife would have cowed them."

"You spoke of a witness," said Harada sharply.

"A man more greedy than the rest. I knew there would have to be such a one and took steps to take him when he appeared."

A pity. Pecula leaned forward in her chair, looking at the accused. He stood tall and calm, his face impassive, the lines and planes firm and strong. There was a strength about him, a hard determination which appealed to her femininity. Tien was strong also, but his strength was of a different kind. A thing of impatience and bluster, quick action and ruthless drive. Would he have killed a beast, knowing the penalties and the risks of betrayal?

She doubted it. He was not a gambler, his nature unable to calculate odds and chances. For him was the steady building, the setting of stone upon stone, each step taken only after inward searching. Anger, always ready to burst into flame, was his only weakness.

Avorot said, as if reading her mind, "You took a chance, Dumarest. Another day, a week at the most, and you would have been in the clear. A gamble you took and lost."

But one which wasn't yet over. Cran was dead, his body safe from pain, his tongue from betrayal. The other?

Dumarest said, coldly, "You spoke of a witness. As yet he hasn't appeared."

"There is no need. His testimony was given and recorded. Now, why not confess and save us all time? A full admission of your guilt may earn mercy from Owner Harada."

"Mercy? My bull slaughtered and you talk of mercy?" Tien's voice was an angry rumble. "If this man is guilty he will suffer the full penalty."

"If? Owner Harada, there is no doubt."

"And no proof," said Pacula quickly. "Where is the witness?"

Avorot said reluctantly, "He is dead, but—"

"Dead?" Tien rose, massive, his face mottled with rage. "Is this a game you are playing with me, Commissioner? Are you shielding those responsible? Owners who—"

"I represent the law," snapped Avorot sharply. "I do not take bribes or yield to influence. My only concern is in discovering the truth. It may not always be palatable, Owner Harada, but must be accepted. I've told you what happened to your beast. The man taken is dead but, as I was about to add, his testimony was given before a witness. One whose word, surely, you will accept. Owner Labria?"

For the first time Usan spoke. She said slowly, "What do you want me to say, Commissioner?

"The truth. You were with me when I questioned the man. Tell Owner Harada what he said."

"He mumbled. He said something about killing a beast."

"And?"

"That's all I heard, Commissioner."

"What?" He stared at her, incredulous. "You were there, standing at my side, listening. You must have heard what was said."

"I heard only a mumble," she insisted. "I cannot lie when a man's life is at stake."

A lie in itself, and Avorot knew it, knew also that Harada would never accept his unsupported word. The man suspected that he was shielding others and only irrefutable proof would convince him otherwise. What game was the woman playing? What was Dumarest to her?

He said tightly, "My lady, I will ask you again. When I questioned the dying man what did he say?"

"I've told you."

"He mentioned a name. He spoke of how the beast was killed. You know it. You were there."

"I heard him mention no name," she said. "And I am not accustomed to having my word doubted, Commissioner. I have no doubt the beast was killed for food, as you say, but there is no evidence against this man."

A wall he couldn't break and a failure he was forced to accept—the taste of it was sour in his mouth. He had been made to look inefficient and a fool and Harada would be slow to forgive if he forgave at all. Avorot looked at the man standing beyond his desk.

Dumarest said, "Am I free to leave?"

"No." The case had taken on an added dimension and who could tell what deeper probing might reveal? "You will be held for further investigation."

"But not in jail." Usan Labria rose, her tone commanding.

"Play the inquisitor if you must, Commissioner, but spare the innocent. I will take charge of this man. Release him in my custody."

"Owner Harada, do you object?"

"Why should I? If he is innocent what does it matter? If he is guilty I know where to find him." Tien's voice deepened. "Make sure that I do, Owner Labria."

"You threaten me, Tien?"

"Take it as you will. Pacula, let us go. We have already wasted too much time on this farce."

Dumarest watched them leave, Avorot in attendance, then looked at the painted face of the old woman. Gently she touched a square of fabric to her lips.

"Let us understand each other," she said. "If you want to run there is little I can do to stop you, but you will never leave this world if you do. Any attempt you make to escape will be held as admission of your guilt. If caught you will be flayed and staked out in the sun."

"Do you think I am guilty, my lady?"

"I know you are."

"Then—"

"Why did I lie?" Her shrug was expressive. "What is Harada's bull to me? And I can use you. There is someone I want you to meet. His name is Sufan Noyoka and we dine with him tonight."

Chapter 4

He was a small man with a large, round head and eyes which gleamed beneath arched and bushy brows. His skin was a dull olive, pouched beneath the chin, sagging beneath the eyes. Like the woman he was old, but unlike her, had none of the stolidity of age. His eyes were like those of a bird, forever darting from place to place, he tripped rather than walked, and his words flowed like the dancing droplets of a fountain.

"Earl! I am delighted you could accept my humble invitation. Usan, my dear, you look as radiant as ever. An amusing episode?" He grinned as the woman told what had happened. "Tien will not be pleased and, to be honest, I cannot blame him. That bull was dear to his heart. You should have been more selective, Earl. I may call you that?"

"If it pleases you, my lord."

"Such formality! Here we are all friends. Some wine? An aperitif before the meal? You wish to bathe? My house is yours to command."

Ancient hospitality, which Dumarest knew better than to accept at face value as he knew better than to accept the man for what he seemed.

Sufan Noyoka was, in many ways, an actor. A man who scattered conversational gambits as a farmer would scatter seed, watching always for an interesting reaction, ready to dart on it, to elaborate and expound, to probe and question. A man who used words as a mask for his thoughts, his apparent foolishness a defense cultivated over the years. To such a man much would be forgiven and his physical frailty would protect him from a challenge. A dangerous man, decided Dumarest, the more so because of his seeming innocence.

"When strangers meet who should be friends, a toast is appropriate," said Sufan. "Usan, my dear, perform the honors.

27

Earl, when you killed that bull did you rely on luck or base your plan on judgment?"

"My lord?"

"You are cautious—that is wise, and the question was stupid. Luck had nothing to do with it. You have hunted in your time?"

"Yes."

"For food, of course, and for profit also, I imagine." Sufan accepted the glass the woman offered to him. It was small, elaborately engraved, filled with a pungent purple fluid. "A liqueur of my own devising, the recipe of which I found in an old book and adapted to local conditions. I had hoped to create a demand, but the essential herbs are scarce and I am too self-indulgent to sell that which I find so appealing. "Usan, your health! Earl, to a long and pleasant association!"

The purple liquid held a smoldering fire, which stung the back of the throat and sent warmth from the stomach. Dumarest sipped, watching as the others drank, emptying his glass only when they had finished. An act of caution which Sufan Noyoka noted and admired.

"Earl," he said, "tell me a little about yourself. What brought you to Teralde?"

"The name."

"Of this world?" Sufan frowned. "It is a name, a label as are all names, but what of that? Were you looking for something? A friend? An opportunity to gain wealth? If so, you chose badly, as by now you are aware. There is little wealth on Teralde."

And what there was remained fast in the grip of jealous Owners. Dumarest looked at his empty glass, then at his host. A shrewd man who could have traveled and who must have known others who had. A chance, small but it had to be taken. Who could tell where the answer was to be found?

"I was looking for a place," said Dumarest. "A planet. My home world."

"Earth?" Usan Labria frowned. "Is there such a place? Sufan?"

"If there is I have never heard of it." The man crossed to a cabinet and took a thick almanac from a shelf, Dumarest waited as he studied it, knowing what he would find. "No such world is listed."

"Which means that it doesn't exist." Usan Labria helped herself to more of the pungent liqueur and took a pill from a small box she produced from a pocket. Swallowing it, she sipped and stood for a moment tense with strain. Then, relaxing, she added, "Earth? Why not call it dirt or sand? How can any world have such a name?"

"My world has it, my lady. And it exists, that I can swear. I was born on it." Dumarest looked at his hand. It was tight around the glass, the knuckles white, tendons prominent with strain. Deliberately he relaxed his grip, accepting the disappointment as he had been forced to accept it so often in the past. "It exists," he said again. "And one day I will find it."

"A quest." Sufan Noyoka refilled the empty glass. "My friend, we have much in common, but more of that later. Yet I think that each man must have a reason for living, for why else was he given imagination? To live to eat, to breed, and to die—that is for animals. But why Teralde? The names are not even similar."

"Earth has another name," said Dumarest. "Terra."

"Terra? I—" Sufan broke off, his eyes shifting, darting, little gleams of reflection turning them into liquid pools. "Teralde," he said musingly. "I see the association. But legend has it that the name originated with Captain Lance Terraim, who was among the first to settle here."

"From where?"

"Who can tell?" Sufan shrugged. "It was long ago and time distorts meaning. Even his family no longer exists and there have been many changes. The land-war of two centuries ago broke the old pattern and the ancient records were lost. I am sorry, my friend, but it seems that you came on a hopeless errand. Teralde is not the world you seek."

As Dumarest had known from the first, yet Sufan's eyes had betrayed him. He knew of Terra, the name at least, and he could know more. But he gave Dumarest no chance to ask questions.

"Let me show you my house, Earl. Usan, my dear, will you arrange the setting of the table? Now come with me, my friend, and tell me what you think of my few treasures. I have an artifact found on Helgeit which holds a mystery and another discovered on a barren world which is equally as strange. You have seen such things in your travels? Have you been to Anilish? Vendhart?" And then, without change of tone, he said, "How often have you killed?"

"My lord?"

"Can you kill?"

"When I have to, yes."

"That is good. Perhaps later you will tell me of your adventures. Now look at this. And this. And what do you think of that?"

The place was partly a museum. Dumarest watched as the man took items from cabinets, his thin hands caressing shapes of stone and distorted metal, old books and moldering scrolls, a crystal which sang as he pressed it, a gem that blazed with a shifting rainbow to the heat of his cupped palm.

For a moment he stared at it then flung it without warning. Dumarest caught it inches from his face.

"Fast," said Sufan. "The reports did not lie. You have unusual reflexes, my friend. Can you handle weapons? A rifle? A laser?"

"Yes."

"And others? A spear? A bow? A sling?"

"Why do you ask, my lord?"

"Still the formality, Earl?" Sufan Noyoka tilted his head as if he were a bird examining a crumb. "A defense," he mused. "A traveler needs to ensure that he does not unwittingly offend local mores and what better way than being always courteous to those who could do him harm? Some would mistake it for servility, but I know better. You have questions you would like to ask?"

"Yes, and have answered."

"Such as?"

"Terra. You have heard the name."

Sufan blinked then said dryly, "An odd request. I would have thought you would be curious as to your own welfare. The reason you are here, for example, and what will happen to you. Yet you ask only after a name. Is your quest, then, so important?"

A gong echoed before Dumarest could answer and his host turned to relock the cabinets that held his treasures. Smiling, he said, "The meal is about to be served and good food should not wait on conversation. Shall we pay it our respects?"

The food was good but Dumarest ate little, choosing dishes high in protein content and barely touching the wine. Pacula Harada had joined then. She wore white, a shimmering gown which graced her figure and robbed her of accumulated years, an illusion accentuated by the soft lighting.

The talk was casual, yet contained undercurrents of which Dumarest was aware, seeming banalities shielding matters of high importance to those at the table. Again Usan Labria took one of her pills, shrugging as Pacula asked after her health.

"I live, girl, what more can I ask?" Then, to Sufan Noyoka, "Well?"

"You were right, my dear."

"You have found the man?" Pacula caught her breath. "I thought as much. Has he agreed?"

"As yet, no."

"Why not? Sufan, you must—"

"Convince him?" He was bland, his smile a mask. "Of course, but gently, my dear. Earl is not a man to be rushed. First he must recognize the situation. Have you further word from Avorot?"

"He is sending men to search the wilderness and others to comb the Warren. Tien demands new evidence and the Commissioner has promised to supply it. If he does not he will be replaced."

"As I expected." Sufan Noyoka toyed with his goblet. "And, if all else fails, he will resort to harsher measures: the use of drugs and electronic probes to wring the truth from a stubborn mind. The Owners will insist on it to avoid a war. Earl, my friend, your time is limited. I mention it only to make the situation clear. Some more wine?"

"No."

"As you wish." Sufan leaned back in his chair, his face bland. "The meat was dried," he mused, "which means a camp was set up in the wilderness. Traces could be found. Your associates will be discovered and will betray you for promise of immunity and reward. Tien will not believe them, but the probes will reveal the truth. Without a vessel, Earl, you are stranded and helpless. You agree?"

"Not helpless," said Usan Labria sharply. "I shall help him, for one."

"To do what, my dear? Hide in the mountains, living on what he can find? Earl could survive, I have no doubt, but only as a savage. And if you defy Tien, what then?"

The woman had already saved his life with her lies; to ask more was to ask too much. Dumarest said flatly, "I think it time we came to the point. Why was I invited here? What do you want from me?"

"Your help," said Pacula quickly. "We need you. I, that is we, can't—Sufan?"

"I will explain, my dear." The man helped himself to more wine, his manner casual, only the slight trembling of his hand betraying his inner tension. "Earl, have you ever heard of Balhadorha?"

"The Ghost World?"

"That is what some call it."

"A legend," said Dumarest. "A myth. A planet which orbits some unknown star in some unknown region of space. There is supposed to be a city or something filled with riches. A fabulous treasure."

"And more," said Pacula. "So much more."

Stuff compounded of dreams and wistful longings. Rumors augmented in taverns and on lonely worlds by men who built a structure of fantasy. The Ghost World, the planet no one could ever find or, having found it, would never leave. The answer to all privation and hurt, a never-never place in which pain had no part and the only tears were those of happiness. Balhadorha—another name for Heaven.

"You don't believe in it," said Usan Labria sharply. "Why not?"

"My lady, every tavern is filled with men who will talk of fabulous worlds. Some of them will even offer to sell you the coordinates. El Dorado, Jackpot, Bonanza, Celdoris—"

"Earth?"

"Earth is not a legend, madam."

"So you say, but who will agree? A name, a world, one in which you believe, but one not listed and totally unknown. Yet you insist that it is real. You even claim to have been born there."

"So?"

"Balhadorha is real. The Ghost World exists. I know it!"

Faith, not knowledge. The desperate need to believe despite all evidence to the contrary. Dumarest looked at the raddled features, the veined, quivering hands, the sick, hurt look in the eyes.

Gently he said, "You could be right, my lady. Space is huge and filled with a billion worlds. No man can know them all."

"Then you admit it could be there?"

"Perhaps. I have heard nothing but wild rumors from those who heard them from others. I have never found it myself."

"But you would be willing to look?" Pacula leaned forward across the table, careless of the glass she sent falling to spill a flood of ruby wine. "You would not object to that?"

She, too, radiated a desperate intensity and Dumarest wondered why. Those who owned wealth and priviledge had little cause to chase a dream. The heaven Balhadorha offered was already theirs; only to the poor and desperate did such fantasies hold magic.

Sufan Noyoka? The man was contained, leaning back in his chair, his face bland; only the eyes, bright with restless dartings, placed him at one with the others.

A question was asked, Earl," he said quietly. "As yet you have made no answer."

To search for a planet he was certain did not exist. To join them in their illusion—but to refuse would gain him nothing but their enmity.

"No, my lady," he said slowly. "I would not object."

"Then it is settled." Usan Labria reached for wine, the decanter making small chimes as it rapped against the edge of her glass. Noyoka was less precipitate.

"A moment, my dear," he said softly. "A man cannot promise to accomplish what he does not understand. Not a man I would be willing to trust. And trust, in this matter, is essential."

"I trust him, Sufan!"

"And I!" Pacula looked at Dumarest. "Do you agree to help us?"

"If I can, my lady. What would it entail?"

"A journey. It may be long and it could be hard."

"We need a man." Usan Labria was more direct. "One who can kill if necessary. A special type of man to take care of what needs to be done. Tell him, Sufan. Explain." Her voice rose a little. "And for God's sake let us be on our way. Already we have waited too long!"

The room was small, filled with the musty odor of ancient books, scraps of oddly shaped material lying on the scarred surface of rough tables. Star maps hung against the walls and the desk bore a litter of papers.

"Let us talk of legends," said Sufan Noyoka. Alone he had guided Dumarest to the room, leading the way up winding stairs to the chamber set beneath the roof. "They are romantic tales embellished and adorned, things of myth and imagination, and yet each could contain a kernel of truth. Eden, for example—you have heard of it?"

"Yes."

"A world of pure joy in which men and women live gracious lives. None need to work. There is no poverty, no pain, no hurt. Each day is a spring of fabulous happiness. Once men owned it, now it is lost. Tell me, do you consider it to be real?"

"Perhaps. I have visited a world with such a name."

"And found what?" Sufan did not wait for an answer. "A desert," he said. "A barren, harsh world of arid soil and acid seas. A lie—the name used only to attract settlers. I, too, have visited Eden and there is more than one world with such a name. But does that mean that the Eden of legend did not, at one time, exist? As Earth, perhaps, once existed?"

"Earth is not a legend."

"So you say, and I will not argue with you, but if you believe in one legend then why not two?"

"Balhadorha," said Dumarest. "The Ghost World."

"Balhadorha." Sufan Noyoka moved to a table and lifted a distorted scrap of metal. "This cost me the labor of a serf for a year. A scrap of debris, you would think, but the composition is something we cannot repeat. A mystery, and there are others, perhaps—later we shall talk about them. For now let me explain what we intend."

"To take a ship and go searching for a legend," said Dumarest. "To follow a dream."

"You think I am mad?" Sufan shrugged. "There are many who think that. But consider a moment. You seek Earth—how do you go about it?" Again he did not wait for an answer. "You ask, you probe, you assemble clues, you sift evidence. From a mountain of rumor you winnow a nodule of fact. To it you add others, always sifting, checking, questioning. Decades of searching and then, with luck, you have the answer."

Light flared as he touched the switch of a projector and, on a screen, glowed the depiction of a sector of space. Stars blazing with a variety of colors, sheets and curtains of luminescence and, in the center, the sprawling blob of a cloud of interstellar dust.

"The Hichen Cloud." An adjustment and it dominated the screen. "An unusual configuration which adopts a different guise when viewed from various positions. It has never been truely explored."

And with reason. Dumarest knew of the conflicting forces which were common in such areas; the electronic vortexes which could take a vessel and render it into a mass of unrecognizable wreckage, the spacial strains which negated the drive of the generators, the psychological stresses which turned men insane.

"You expect to find Balhadorha in that?"

"The prospect disturbs you?"

"Yes." Dumarest was blunt. "I've had experience with such areas. "Only a fool would venture into such a region. No sane captain would dare risk his vessel and no crew be willing to take the chance."

"A normal captain and a normal crew, I agree. But you underestimate the power of greed, my friend. Think of what could be gained. Wealth beyond imagination, the treasure of a world, gems and precious metals—" Sufan Noyoka broke off as he saw Dumarest's expression. "Such things do not tempt you?"

"Do they you?"

"No. A man can only eat so much, live in one place at a time, wear one suit of clothing. But even so, wealth has power. Think of it, my friend. The power to travel where and when you will. To buy a ship to aid you in your search. Money to ease the path to a thousand worlds. You killed a beast in order to live and risked your life in so doing. Why not risk it again for much, much more?"

The voice of temptation, and Dumarest was aware of the man's subtlety. Sufan knew more than he had admitted, in small ways he had betrayed himself and, though no threat had been made, always it was implied. A word and he would be delivered to Avorot, to be kept in jail, to wait until evidence had accumulated or the probes were brought into use.

The trap which had closed had not yet opened and would not until he left this world.

"You will need a ship," he said. "A ship and a crew."

"All has been arranged." Sufan's voice, dry as the rustle of windblown leaves, held no emotion, but his eyes, for a moment, ceased their restless dancing. "This is no casual whim. For years I have planned, each step taken with painstaking care, units assembled to form a composite whole. Only one thing was lacking and you provide it."

"A bodyguard?"

"That and more." Sufan Noyoka drew in his breath, his chest rising, his eyes blazing with a brighter shine. "Soon we shall be on our way, and think, my friend, of what you might find."

The answer to his long, long search, perhaps. The exact location of Earth. On Balhadorha, so rumor claimed, the answers to all things could be found.

Chapter 5

Each morning, now, it was harder to wake, the time in which she lay, conscious only of pain, lengthening so that the days became shorter and life ran like sand from a container, each grain another precious hour. And yet, now, there were compensations, and lying in the shade of an awning, Usan Labria considered them, savoring them as she waited for the pills to take effect.

It was good to be in the open. Good to breathe deeply of the clean air and to feel the sun. Best of all was to know that she was not alone, that with her was someone who cared. Not for herself as a woman, but for herself as a person. More she could not expect, much as she would have liked it, but later perhaps, when she was free of pain and things were as she hoped—who could tell?

A dream and she knew it, but it was a nice one and it did no harm to dream. Less to relax and to let another take care of things, and Dumarest had proved to be a good companion.

"My lady?" He stood in the opening of the shelter, limned by the sunlight, which threw a nimbus of light around him while casting his face in shadow. "Is there anything you need?"

"A little water." It was close at hand but to be served was an added pleasure.

She sipped, taking another pill, then looking up, met his eyes.

"Do you think I'm a fool?"

"No, my lady."

"Call me Usan, Earl, and be honest. Am I?"

"No. To hope is not to be foolish."

"Others would not agree with you. My cousin for one." Memory of him thinned her lips. "He can't wait for me to die so that he can inherit. Much good will it do him. My lands are mortgaged to the hilt, the beasts sold, the house

37

needing repair. Everything I own has been turned into money and I've borrowed all I could. A last fling, Earl, and still you say I am not a fool?"

"Would it matter if I did?"

He was blunt and she liked that, liked too his air of assurance, his smooth competence. Raoul had once been like that, or so she had thought, but that had been long, long ago. He was dead now as were others she had once called friend or lover. And the thing which had struck her had driven still more away. None like to be associated with illness and her manner hadn't helped. Well, to hell with them; soon, with luck, she would have the last laugh.

"Sit beside me," she ordered. "Talk to me, Earl. You have nothing else to do."

"The area must be checked, my lady."

"Usan—we are friends are we not?"

"The area must still be checked."

"Why? Are you afraid Avorot will find us here? What if he does? I have a right to go camping and you are in my charge." Her voice, she knew, was becoming querulous. Deliberately she deepened it, made it harsh. "Do as I say, man. You have nothing to fear."

For a moment Dumarest stared at her, scenting the odor which was strong in the shelter, the scent of decaying tissue exuded through the skin. Internal organs rotting, afflicted with a disease local medicine could not cure. She was dying and knew it but struggled to the last. An attribute he could appreciate.

"Later, Usan. Later."

Sufan Noyoka had planned well. The ship he had summoned would call at the field, pick him up together with Pacula Harada, then light to land again in this spot he had chosen. The only way to avoid the search Avorot would be certain to make. Usan Labria had to stay with him; alone she would not have been allowed to embark.

A responsibility Dumarest could have done without. The delay had been too long. Suspicion must have been aroused, a search launched, and others would have spotted the raft in which they had traveled.

Leaving the shelter Dumarest climbed to the summit of a mound. All around stretched the broken terrain of the foothills, the loom of mountains rising like a wall to the north. An arid place, as bad as the wilderness which ran beyond the city to the south, dotted only with clumps of thorny scrub. A bleak area into which they had brought food and water and supplies—things which were getting low.

Narrowing his eyes, Dumarest searched the sky. It was clear, touched only with patches of fleecy cloud, long streamers showing the presence of a wind high in the stratosphere. Turning, he looked toward the camp. The shelter was made of fabric the color of the ground, invisible to a casual eye, but any searching raft could be equipped with infrared scanners which would signal their body heat.

"Earl!" He heard the woman cry out as he neared the shelter. "Earl!"

She was crouched on her cot, one hand fumbling at her sleeve, at the laser she carried there. Her eyes were wide as she stared at the thing a foot from the edge of her cot. A small, armored body, the chitin a glossy ocher, the legs thin and hooked, the mandibles wide. A creature three inches long, which lived beneath the sand, coming out only at night, attracted by the water she had spilled. A thing relatively harmless, inedible, but with a sting which could burn like acid.

It died as the thrown knife speared through the thorax, writhing, crushing as Dumarest slammed down the heel of his boot.

"Earl! I—"

"It's dead. Forget it."

"Yes." No child, a woman of experience, she felt a momentary shame at her panic. "It startled me. I was dozing and woke and saw it. Two years ago I would have ignored it. A year ago and I would have burned it." She looked at her hands and added bitterly, "Now even my fingers refuse to obey me. Age, Earl, the curse of us all. Couple it with disease and where is our dignity?"

He made no answer, kicking the crushed body of the insect from the shelter. As he wiped the knife she reached out and took it from his hand. It was heavy, the blade nine inches long, the edge sweeping to meet the reverse curve from the back, the point needle-sharp at the union. The hilt was worn, the guard scarred, the edge honed to a razor finish.

"And with this you killed a bull," she said. "And men too?"

"When necessary."

"Men who tried to kill you? Those who sought your life?"

He took the knife and slipped it into his boot, then stepped again to the open front of the shelter. The sky was still clear of any dangerous fleck—all that could be seen of a high-flying raft.

"Life," said the woman bleakly as he turned. "The most precious thing there is, because without it there is nothing. That is what Balhadorha means to me. With money enough to bribe them the surgeons of Pane will cure my ills. Given a fortune they could even be persuaded to transplant my brain into a new, young body. I have heard it is possible." She paused, waiting for his reassurance, then said sharply. "You think it possible?"

"Perhaps."

"And don't agree with it? The monks don't. I talked to Brother Vray and he was against it. He advised me to accept what had to come and pointed out that even if the surgeons could supply a new body, it would be at the expense of another's life. He told me to have faith. Faith!" Her voice was bitter. "What is faith to me? What matter if a thousand should die so that I might live? I—Earl!"

He supported her as she slumped, one arm around her shoulders, her head resting against his chest. Her skin was livid, the lips blue, the eyes stark with fear.

"Your pills," he snapped. "Which?"

"A blue," she panted. "And a white. Quickly!"

He thrust them between her lips and rubbed her throat to make her swallow. Relief came quickly, the flaccid skin showing a tinge of red, the eyes clearing from the haze of pain to become misted with chemically induced tranquillity.

"Sleep," she whispered. "I must sleep. But don't leave me, Earl. You promise?"

"I promise."

She sighed like a child and settled against him, one hand rising, the thin fingers clutching at his own. Her voice was a susurration, thoughts vocalized without conscious thought.

"I don't want you ever to leave me, Earl. I want you to stay with me for always. When I get my new, young body I will show you the real meaning of love. You will be proud of me then. I will make you a king." Then, as the sky split with a crash of sound, she murmured, more loudly, "Thunder, Earl. It's thunder. We are going to have a storm."

She was wrong. The sound was that of a ship coming to land.

Standing before his desk Ibius Avorot listened to the even modulation of a voice asking questions and answered each with truth. More and he replied with lies. As the voice fell silent he said, "Well?"

"Your equipment seems to be in order."

"As I claimed."

Cyber Khai made no comment, none was needed. The Commissioner was intelligent enough to have made checks and the test had been only to prove his veracity. Standing behind the desk where he had seen the signals of the lie detector he made a warm splash of color in the cold bleakness of the room. Tall, dressed in a scarlet robe, the breast emblazoned with the Seal of the Cyclan, he seemed both more and less than human.

There was a coldness about the face, the cheeks sunken, the bone prominent, the skull shaved to accentuate the likeness to a skull. A face which betrayed no emotion, for the cyber could feel none. Taken when young, taught, trained, an operation performed on his brain, he was incapable of anger, fear, hate, greed—the gamut of human desires. The only pleasure he could know was that of mental achievement. His sole ambition was to serve the organization to which he belonged. The Cyclan which, one day, would dominate the entire galaxy.

Avorot said, "There is no mistake. The man is Earl Dumarest. How did you know he was here?"

"The prediction of his reaching this world was in the order of ninety-two percent probability once it was known he had left Laconde. Are you certain he did not leave on the vessel which had just departed?"

"Positive. I made a complete search."

"Including cargo?"

"Yes." Avorot added bleakly, "I have my own reasons for not wanting him to escape."

The loss of his position and the ruin of his career, but it was a matter which could be easily handled. The anger of the Owner concerned could be nullified with the offer of the service of the Cyclan. His own greed would make him accept the bargain and, once a cyber had been established, another step would have been taken to ensure the success of the Master Plan. Teralde was a poor world of jealous factions, one which posed no real problem and one of small gain, but if necessary it would be done.

Khai touched a control and listened to the recorded voices
of the interrogation. Avorot had been a fool, not once had he
asked a direct question as to guilt and Dumarest must have
known that his physical reactions were being monitored to
determine the truth of his answers. A matter he did not mention, the episode was past and recriminations would serve no
useful purpose.

"The woman," he said. "Usan Labria. Why did you allow
her to take the man into her custody?"

"I had no choice. Also I hoped to discover an association
between them. There had to be a reason for her lies."

"And have your informants reported?" There would have
to be spies, otherwise Avorot could not have hoped to gain
information. As the Commissioner hesitated Khai said again,
"Have they?"

"No. The woman is not at home. She left with Dumarest
that same evening and neither has been seen since."

"And she was not on the vessel which left?"

"No. Sufan Noyoka and Pacula Harada but not her and
not the man. Both must still be on this world. The woman is
old and ill, soon they will have to make an appearance, and
when they do, I'll arrest Dumarest and hold him for judgment."

The man was compounding his folly, blinded by his own
limitations. Dumarest was not an ordinary man, something he
should have realized from the first, and to plan as if he would
act like one was to insult his intelligence. Yet the man was
not wholly to blame. He did not have the ingrained attribute
of any cyber, the ability to take a handful of facts, correlate
them, extrapolate from a known situation to predict the logical sequence of events.

"Where did Usan Labria take Dumarest after she left her
house? To that of Sufan Noyoka? And he with another left
on the ship?"

"Yes," said Avorot. "But what has that to do with it?"

The cyber's voice did not change from its smooth, even
modulation, tones designed to eliminate all irritant factors,
but Avorot inwardly cringed as he listened to the obvious.

"Dumarest and the woman left the city and must now be
in hiding somewhere. There was an association between them
and those who left on the vessel. It was obvious you would
make a search. Therefore the prediction that they expect to

be picked up at some other place by the ship is in the order of ninety-eight percent."

"Not certainty?"

"Nothing is or can be certain, Commissioner. Always there is the unknown factor to be taken into consideration. Bring me maps of the immediate area and have your men check on the movements of all rafts during the period since the interrogation."

Fifteen minutes later they were in the air, flying toward the north and the loom of distant mountains. The cyber had selected three places as probable sites and at the second they found it. Even as they fell to land Avorot knew they were too late.

Bleakly he looked at the shelter, the crushed body of the insect. The fact it was still visible showed how close they had been; nothing edible was left by the scavengers for long.

That evening the sky flamed with color but Cyber Khai saw none of it. The pleasure it gave to normal men held no magic for him as neither did food and wine and sweet perfumes. Food was nothing but fuel to maintain the efficiency of the body—his gauntness was due not to deprivation but to an elimination of wasteful fat and water-heavy tissue. A flesh-and-blood robot, he was concerned only with the determination of the logical sequence of events.

Again Dumarest had escaped, the unknown factor of luck and circumstances which worked so well on his behalf augmenting his innate cunning. Even now he was on a ship traversing the void—heading where?

Given an intelligence large enough, a single leaf would yield the pattern of the tree on which it had grown, the planet on which it stood, the shape of the universe to which it belonged. Khai was not so ambitious; he would be content if the trained power of his mind could predict the world to which the ship was bound.

Seated in Avorot's office he assembled scraps and fragments of data; the name of the vessel, the number of its crew, the tally of those it carried. From the Commissioner's spies he learned more; casual words, idle gossip, and finally, a name.

"Balhadorha." Avorot frowned. He sat at a communicator from which he relayed information. "I've heard of it. The Ghost World."

"A place of legend," said Khai evenly. "It's whereabouts is unknown unless those in the vessel have learned of it."

A chilling thought. Space was vast and journeys could be long. Without a guide any planet in the galaxy could be its final destination. He needed more.

Yethan Ctonat provided it. He entered the office, smiling, bland, his eyes shifting from the cyber to Avorot, from the Commissioner back to the figure in the scarlet robe.

"My lord!" His bow was humble. "It has come to my ears that you are in some small difficulty. It may be within my power to aid you. You are interested in Sufan Noyoka?"

"Yes. What do you know?"

"Perhaps little, but a man in my position hears odd items, and at times I have been entrusted with various commissions. They could have no meaning, of course, but who knows in what scrap of information the truth may lie?"

"What do you know, man?" Avorot was impatient. "Speak or waste no more of our time!"

The Hausi stiffened, an almost imperceptable gesture which the cyber recognized. Despite his demeanor the man had pride.

Khai said, "You wish to speak to me in private? Commissioner, if you will be so kind? During your absence perhaps you will compile a total list of the cargo the ship carried. And I would be interested to know exactly what was left in the shelter we found."

Small errands, but they would salve his pride, and from him had been learned all of use. As the door closed behind the rigidly stiff back of the officer the cyber said, "Well?"

"A small matter first, my lord. If my information should be of value?"

"You will be rewarded. A prediction as to the immediate future of the market in chelach meat."

It was enough, the service of a cyber at no cost and information which could lead to an easy fortune. Taking a step closer to the desk the Hausi lowered his voice.

"Sufan Noyoka is an unusual man. For years he has been interested in things out of this world. By that I mean his interests lie elsewhere. His lands are poor, his herd depleted, yet he is not the fool many take him to be. Goods have been converted into money. Friends have been made."

He went on, telling of things the cyber already knew, but he made no interruption, knowing the man was merely trying to inflate his importance. And verification was always of value. Only when the agent had finished did he speak.

"Are you certain?"

"My lord, why should I lie? I handled the matter myself."

"The Hichen Cloud?"

"All available maps of the area together with reports from those who had either penetrated the Cloud or who had ventured close. I sold him an artifact, a thing of mystery, one found on a wrecked vessel discovered by a trader."

The Hichen Cloud! It was enough. After the Hausi had left, gratified with his prediction, the cyber rose and stepped into an inner room. It was one used by Avorot when working late and contained little aside from a cot and toilet facilities.

Locking the door Khai rested supine on the couch, resting his fingers on the wide band locked around his left wrist. A device which, when activated, ensured that no scanner or electronic spy could focus on his vicinity. Like the locked door it was an added precaution; even if someone had stood at his side they would have learned nothing.

Relaxing, he closed his eyes and concentrated on the Samatchazi formulae. Imperceptibly he lost the affinity with the sensory apparatus of his body. Had he opened his eyes he would have been blind. Closed in the womb of his skull his brain ceased to be irritated by external stimuli, the ceaseless impact of irrelevant data impossible to avoid while in a wholly conscious state. Isolated, it became a thing of pure intellect, its reasoning awareness untrammeled. Only then did the grafted Homochon elements become active. Rapport was immediate."

Khai became vibrantly alive.

A life in which it seemed every door in the universe had opened to emit a flood of light. Light which was the pure essence of truth, flooding his being, permeating his every cell. He was the living part of an organism which stretched across endless space in a profusion of glittering nodes, each node the pulse of an intelligent mind. All were interconnected with shimmering filaments, a glinting web reaching to infinity. He saw it, was a part of it while it was a part of himself, sharing yet owning the tremendous gestalt of minds.

At the heart of the web glowed the mass of Central Intelligence, the heart of the Cyclan. Buried deep beneath miles of rock on a lonely world, the massed brains absorbed his knowledge as a sponge sucked water. A mental communication in the form of words, quick, almost instantaneous, organic transmission against which that of supra-radio was the merest crawl.

"Dumarest? There is no possibility of doubt?"

"None."

"Your prediction as to present whereabouts?"

"Insufficient data for prediction of high probability but certainly in the direction of the Hichen Cloud. Other factors, unkown to me, may have important bearing."

A moment in which he sensed the interchange of a million diverse items of information, facts correlated, assessed, a decision reached. The multiple intelligence doing what one brain alone could never achieve.

And then, *"Chamelard. Word will be sent. Follow."*

That was all.

The rest was sheet intoxication, which filled him with a pleasure beyond the scope of ordinary flesh.

Always it was the same during the period when the Homochon elements sank again into quiescence and the machinery of the body began to realign itself with metal control. Like a disembodied spirit Khai drifted in an empty darkness while he sensed and thrilled to strange memories and unlived experiences; the overflow of other minds, the emission of unknown intelligences. The aura which radiated from the tremendous cybernetic complex which was the unifying force of the Cyclan.

One day he would be a part of it. His body would age and his senses lose their sharp edge, but his mind would remain as active as ever. A useful tool not to be lost. Then he would be taken and his intelligence rid of the hampering constraints of flesh. His brain, removed, would join the others to pulse in nutrient fluid, hooked in a unified whole, all working to a common end.

The complete and absolute control of the entire galaxy. The elimination of waste and the direction of effort so that every man and every world would become the parts of a universal machine.

Chapter 6

Death had come very close and Usan Labria knew it. Now, lying on the cot, she savored every breath, the touch of the blanket which covered her, even the soft vibration of the Erhaft Field, which sent the vessel hurtling through space at a speed much faster than that of light. To feel. To know that she was alive. Alive!"

Looking down at her Dumarest said, "How are you, Usan?"

"Earl!" She stared at him with sunken eyes. "You saved my life in the shelter. If you hadn't given me those pills—was I very foolish?"

"No."

"At times they have odd effects. I seem to remember babbling some nonsense."

"Memories of childhood," he lied. "And you thought the sound of the ship landing was that of thunder."

"Yes." She looked at her hands, knowing he was being kind. "Have we been traveling long?"

"A day. You're under quick-time, so be careful."

They were all under quick-time, the magic of the drug slowing their metabolism so that hours became minutes—a convenience to shorten the tedium of the journey.

"I'll remember." Slowly she reared to sit upright, leaning her back against the bulkhead. "So we're finally on our way," she said. "To Balhadorha. What did you hope to gain, Earl? Why did you join us?"

"If you remember, my lady," he said dryly, "I had little choice."

"True, but even so you will share in what we find. An equal share, I shall insist on it." For a moment she fell silent then said, "Earth. I keep remembering the name. Your world, you say, but if you want to return then why not simply book a passage?"

"Because no one seems to know where it lies."

"Then—"

"It exists," he said. "I was born on the planet and I know. I left when a boy, stowing away on a ship, not knowing the risk I ran. The captain was more than kind. He could have evicted me, instead he allowed me to work my passage. And, when he died, I moved on.

World after world, each closer toward the Center, where worlds were thick and commerce heavy. Traveling deeper and deeper into space until even the very name of Earth was unknown. And then the desire to return, to find it again, to search and probe and, always, meeting with the blank wall of failure.

"A quest," she said. "An obsession perhaps, and now your reason for living. But why, Earl? What does it matter if you never find it? Surely there are other worlds on which you can settle? You could marry, have children, build a family. Has there never been one woman who could have won you from your dream?

More than one, but never had more than the temptation lasted. Looking down at her he thought of Lallia, of Derai, of Kalin with the flame-colored hair. Kalin who had loved him and who had given him more than life itself.

The secret for which the Cyclan had hunted him from world to world. Would still be hunting him. Would never cease until they had regained the secret stolen from their laboratory on some isolated world.

The secret which would give the old woman the thing she yearned to possess.

Only he knew the sequence in which the molecular units had to be arranged to form the affinity-twin. Fifteen units, the last reversed to determine dominant or submissive characteristics. A combination which could be found by trial and error, but the possible number of arrangements ran into millions and it would take millennia to make and try them all. Too much time for the Cyclan to contemplate when, once in their hands, the answer could be found.

And, once found, it would give them power incredible in its scope.

The artificial symbiote injected into the bloodstream would nestle in the base of the cortex and take over control of the entire nervous and sensory system. The brain holding the dominant half would mesh with and take over that of the host. The effect, to the dominant mind, would be that it had acquired a new body. Used by the Cyclan the brain of a cyber would reside in each and every person of influence and power. They would be puppets moving to the dictates of the Master Plan.

Power—a bribe no old man would refuse, no old woman could resist. He had it—if Usan Labria knew, would she hesitate to betray him for such a reward?

"Earl?" She frowned as she watched his face. "Your eyes—have I offended you?"

"No. I was thinking of something else."

"A woman?" Her smile was grotesque. "If I were younger I could be jealous. Many women must have envied the one close to your side. Perhaps one day—" She broke off, then ended, "It was good of you to visit me, but I must not take all of your time. Pacula could need attention. You know why she is with us?"

"No. Why?"

"That she will tell you if she wants. Ask her, Earl. Talk to her. She needs someone she can trust."

Sufan Noyoka had done well. Dumarest had expected the ship to be old, scarred, the hull patched, the decks scuffed and the bulkheads grimed, a hulk little better than scrap. Instead, while small, the *Mayna* was clean and in good condition. A vessel a Mangate could have owned or one used by a wealthy family for private transportation. Its cost must have been high—proof of Noyoka's dedication to his ideal as the crew was visible evidence of his power of pursuasion.

A small crew, a captain, a navigator and an engineer. They together with the two women and Noyoka himself formed the complement together with Dumarest and a man who liked to play with cards.

Marek Cognez was a slender man with a spurious appearance of youth, his features finely pointed, the lips full and sensuous. A man almost womanish in the soft richness of his clothing, the delicate bone structure of his face and hands. His fingers were long, tapered, the nails trimmed and polished. A heavy ring glowed on the index finger of each hand, the stones elaborately carved, the bands wide.

He sat at the table in the salon, Pacula at his side, the cards in his hands making a soft rustling noise as he shuffled.

"Come and join us, Earl. A diversion to pass the time."

Pacula said, "How is Usan?"

"Awake. With food and rest she will be on her feet soon."

"Another female to grace the company. Well, any amusement would be welcome. Our captain is engrossed with his instruments and Noyoka keeps our navigator busy with plans and suggestions. A union I find suspicious. If two heads are better than one then should not three be better than two?"

"Your time will come later, Marek," said Pacula. "It doesn't take your genius to cross empty space."

"But to find the answer to a puzzle?" Marek smiled as she made no answer. It held a little genuine amusement. "Well, each to his own. Some to provide money in order to obtain the ship, others to run it, one to discover how time and opportunity can be merged to achieve the desired result. And you, Earl? What is your purpose?"

"Does he need one?" Pacula was sharp and Dumarest sensed she had no liking for the man. "You ask too many questions, Marek."

"How else to gain answers? For all things there is a reason and, knowing them, a pattern can be formed. You, for example, my dear. Why should your brother have thought you bound for Heidah? A lie compounded by Noyoka's hints and agreement. And why should a vessel have landed just before we left carrying a cyber?"

Dumarest said, "Are you sure of that?"

"Can anyone mistake the scarlet robe?" Marek was bland. "A routine visit perhaps, who can tell? The pieces of a puzzle or elements unessential to the pattern? Perhaps the cards will tell."

They made a sharp rapping as he tapped them on the table, shuffled, cut and slowly dealt. Pursing his lips he looked at the exposed card.

"The Lord of Fools. Symbolic, don't you think? On this ship all are fools. But who is the Lord, Earl? Who is the biggest? Can you tell me that?"

His voice was soft yet holding a note of irony as if he expected to be challenged. As if he hoped to be challenged.

Dumarest said, "If you think we are fools then why join us?"

"Because life itself is a game for fools. You doubt it? Consider, my friend, what is the essence of being? We are born, we live for a while, and then, inevitably, we die. Which means, surely, that the object of existence is to reach an end.

Does it matter how soon that end is reached? If the object of a journey is to arrive at a destination then why linger on the way?"

Philosophical musings with which Dumarest had little patience. As he made no answer Pacula said, "Tell us."

"Students kneeling at the feet of a master—my friends, you surprise me. Is it so hard to venture an answer? For the fun of it, try."

"To enjoy the scenery," said Dumarest shortly. "To ease the path for those who follow."

"Which assumes that those who went before cared about us who come after. The facts are against you, my friend." Marek turned another card. "The Queen of Desire. A fit mate for the Lord of Fools. But to which of the women we carry does the card apply? You, Pacula? Or to the one who lies in her cabin engrossed in erotic dreams?"

"How can you say that!" Pacula radiated her anger. "Usan is old and—"

"Have the old no desires?" Marek, unruffled, fired the question. "Why else is she with us? But it seems I tread on delicate ground. Even so, let us ponder the matter. Usan Labria is, as you say, old, but I have seen older toss away their pride and dignity when the demands of the flesh grow too strong. Is she such a one? What do you say, Earl?"

"You had better change the subject."

"And if I do not?" For a moment their eyes met and Pacula felt a sudden tension, broken when, smiling, Marek shrugged and said, "Well, no matter. Earl, shall we play?"

"Later, perhaps."

"A diplomatic reply. Not a refusal, not a promise, simply meaningless words. Do I offend you?"

"No."

"And if I did, would you fight?"

Dumarest said coldly, "Such talk is stupid and you are not a stupid man. Why did you join us?"

"Because life is a game and it is my pleasure to win at games. Balhadorha is a puzzle, a challenge to be solved, and I mean to solve it. Are you answered?"

"For now, yes."

"And our captain. You have met Rae Acilus, what do you think about him? Is he the Lord of Fools?"

The captain, like his ship, was small, compact, neatly clean. A man with hooded eyes and thin lips, his hands alone

instruments of emotion; the fingers twitching sometimes at
rest, more often curled as if to make a fist. A taciturn man
who had said little, accepting Dumarest after a searching
glance of the eyes, having him fill the vacant place of stew-
ard.

"A case could be made for it," continued Marek, touching
the card with a slender finger, light glowing from his ring.
Greed makes fools of us all and Acilus is no exception. He
was ambitious and hoped for rapid gain. He took command
of a ship carrying contract workers to a mining world. A
slave ship in all but name and he saved on essential supplies.
There was an accident, the hull was torn and—can you guess
the rest?"

"Tell me."

Marek shrugged. "Not all could hope to survive. Our captain, faced with a decision, evicted seventy-three men and
women. Naturally they had no suits. Sometimes, when asleep,
he cries out about their eyes."

Truth or a facile lie? Dumarest remembered the man, his
masked face, the way he had held himself, the hands. The
story could be true, such things happened, but true or not it
made little difference. The journey had started, they were on
their way.

He said, "So he hopes to get rich and regain his self-re-
spect. Is that what you are telling me?"

"You are not concerned? Our ship captained by a killer?"

"Is he a good captain?"

"One of the best, but is that your only interest?" Marek
looked thoughtful. "It seems that you have something in common. Let us see what it could be." He touched the cards and
held one poised in his fingers. "Your card, my friend. Which
will it be?"

It fell to lie face upward, the design clear in the light. That
of the Knave of Swords.

Dumarest heard the knock and rose to open the door of
his cabin, stepping back as Pacula Harada stepped inside.
She was pale, her eyes huge in the oval of her face, the small
lines of age making a barely perceptible mesh at their
corners. Beneath the gown she wore her figure was smoothly
lush, the breasts high, the hips wide. A mature woman less
young than she looked, but now one distraught.

"Earl, I must talk to you."

"About what?"

"You. Marek. That card."

"It meant nothing."

"So you say, but how can I be sure? And to whom else can I turn? Sufan is busy and Usan asleep. I feel alone on this ship and vulnerable. I thought I could trust you, now I'm not so sure. Marek—"

"Can you trust him?"

"I don't know. He is brilliantly clever and, I think, a little insane. Perhaps we are all insane. My brother would have no hesitation in saying so. He thinks I am mad. That's why he gave me money to go to Heidah and have my mind treated to remove painful memories. He meant to be kind, but how can he understand? How can anyone?"

"Pacula, be calm."

"I can't. I've been sitting, alone in the dark, thinking, remembering. Culpea, my child! Culpea!"

He caught her as she collapsed in a storm of weeping, guiding her to the cot, forcing her to sit on the edge, dropping beside her with his arm around her shoulders, holding her tight until the emotion climax had passed.

Then, as she dabbed at her eyes, he said quietly, "Culpea?"

"My child. My daughter."

"And?" He gripped her shoulders as she remained silent and turned her to look at him. "Tell me," he demanded. "Tell me."

For her good, not his, a catharsis to ease her inner torment. Hurtful memories, nursed, could fester and gain a false eminence. It was better she should speak and, until she did, he was powerless to say or do anything which could help.

"It was eight years ago," she said dully. "Culpea was four. Tien had brought us both to Teralde after Elim had died. He had never really forgiven my having married a stranger and was glad to get us back where he said we belonged. Perhaps he was right, on Lemach there was little to hold us, just the house, some memories, a grave. Oh, Elim, why did you die?"

A question asked by women since the dawn of time and for which there was no answer. Dumarest waited, patient, silent, his strength not his words giving her the courage to continue.

"Tien was ambitious," she continued, her voice calm now, as dull as before. "He wanted to extend his holdings and we

went with him to examine some land to the east. He wanted
my opinion and we flew on to the foot of the mountains. We
left the others in a second raft, Culpea, her nurse, some
guards. It seemed safe enough, the air was still, and who
would want to injure a child?"

"And?"

"Our examination took longer than expected. The others
must have tried to follow us. We——" She broke off, swallowing. "We found their raft. The nurse was dead, the guards
also, but there was no sign of the child. I searched——God,
how I searched——but found nothing. Eight years," she ended.
"An eternity."

And one on which it would be unwise to brood, the long,
empty years, the hope which never died, the forlorn conviction that, somewhere, somehow, the girl continued to exist.
Dumarest sensed her pain.

He said, "What happened? Did the raft crash?"

"Who knows? We found it broken and wrecked. The nurse
was in a crevass, the guards scattered. None were missing but
all were dead. Tien went to summon help and he and others
combed the area. Nothing was found, but he insisted that
Culpea must have fallen into a crevass. Some of them are
very deep and impossible to investigate."

"But you didn't believe that?"

"No." She straightened, turned, defiant as she met his eyes.
"I think that she still lives. Someone must have taken her.
Sufan——"

"He was there?"

"It was his land we were examining. Later he sold it to
Tien. His raft landed as we searched and he joined us. It was
he who found the nurse."

"And nothing else?" Dumarest explained as she stared
blankly. "Did he spot another raft? Men on foot who could
have had the child with them? No? Was a demand ever made
for ransom?"

A stupid question——if it had, it would have been proof the
girl lived——but he asked it with deliberate intent.

"No," she said reluctantly. "None. Not then or since."

"Which eliminates kidnappers. Did your husband have enemies?"

"No. He was a quiet man. I met him when he came to
Teralde and we left together. Tien was surprised, he had

thought me too old to attract a man, but he made no objection."

"What was his name? What did he do?"

"Elim? He was of the Shalada and worked in the biological institute on Lemach. He came to Teralde with a cargo of genetically mutated chelach. We met at a reception and later in the dark." Her laughter was strained. "It was odd, I couldn't see a thing, but to him the night was as clear as day. He teased me a little, describing how I looked and the movements I made. He was gentle and I was flattered and I loved him. Five years," she said bleakly. "Such a short time for happiness."

"Many have less," said Dumarest. "How did he die?"

"A tumor. He woke crying from the pains in his head and was dead before morning. The doctors said it was a virulent growth of exceptional malignancy. For a while I worried about Culpea, but there was no need. The condition was not hereditary." She inhaled, her chest swelling, her breasts rising beneath her gown. "An old story and one which must bore you. What interest can you have in a lost child?"

He dodged the question. "Is that why you are with us?"

"If Sufan is right Balhadorha will provide all the money I need to continue the search. And I must continue it, Earl. I must know what happened to my child. If she is dead I must find what remains of her body. If alive I must discover where she is. I must!"

"And you will."

"Do you humor me?" She looked at him, face hard, eyes reflecting her anger. "Many have done that. Some men wonder why I did not marry again and have another child. The answer is simple—I cannot. It happens to some women, Earl. One child is all they can bear. That is why Culpea is so important to me—she is the only child I will ever have."

And then, suddenly, her anger broke to leave nothing but a distraught woman blindly reaching for the comfort he could give.

"Earl, help me! For the love of God, help me!"

Chapter 7

Timus Omilcar bent over the exposed interior of the generator and made a minor adjustment. Without looking up he said, "Earl?"

Dumarest called out the readings on the dials set in the console, adding, "That's optimum, Timus."

"And as good as we can get." The engineer straightened, satisfied. Closing and sealing the dust cover of the unit he wiped his hands on a cloth and reached for a bottle. "Join me?"

"Just a little."

"Why be so cautious?" Wine gurgled as the man poured a generous measure into each of two glasses. "On the *Mayna* each man is as good as the next. We're all partners. To success, Earl—by God, it's time some came my way."

He was a big man, thick-set, hair growing in thick profusion on his body and arms, more resting in a tangled mat on his head. Red hair, curled, reflecting the light in russet shimmers. His face was a combination of disaster, the nose squashed, eyebrows scarred, the lobe of one ear missing. An ugly man with the appearance of a brutal clown but whose hands held magic when it came to dealing with machines.

"A half percent added efficiency," he said, lowering his half-empty glass. "So much for those who swore the generator couldn't be improved."

"Who?"

"The engineers on Perilan." He squinted at Dumarest. "You don't know the history of this ship, eh? Interested?"

"No." Dumarest touched the wine to his lips, only pretending to swallow. "Just as long as it gets us to where we want to go."

"And back again," added the engineer. He finished the rest of his wine and poured more. "Don't worry," he said, catching Dumarest's eyes. "This stuff can't hurt me."

"I wasn't thinking about you."

"The ship?" Timus shrugged. "I've never lost one yet despite what they claimed. The generator didn't fail, it was the fool in command, but what is the word of an engineer against that of a master? Well, to hell with it—soon I'll have money to burn."

"Is that why you're with us?"

"Of course." The battered face showed amusement. "What else can anyone hope to obtain from Balhadorha? All this talk of joy unspeakable, of pleasure beyond imagination, a world on which can be found the answer to all problems—that is rubbish for fools. What can a man want that money cannot buy? With enough he can become the king of a world."

A simple ambition and one Dumarest had expected. The engineer at least was uncomplicated and had quickly warmed to friendly overtures, pleased at Dumarest's knowledge of ships and machines. A reaction different from that of the captain, who remained cold and aloof.

As the man sipped his wine Dumarest said casually, "Did you see the cyber who landed on Teralde?"

"No."

"But one did land?"

"It's possible. The other ship bore their seal and the red scum get everywhere. Why, Earl?" Timus narrowed his eyes a little. "What's your interest in the Cyclan?"

"I don't like them."

"You and me both." The engineer glowered at his wine. "I had a good thing going when I was young, then the Manager called in the Cyclan to increase efficiency. Their damned predictions cost me my job, my house, what I had saved, and the girl I intended to marry. You?"

"Something much the same." Dumarest lifted the glass and drank to avoid further explanation. "I'd better check the stores."

"Why? They're safe."

"I'd still better check."

The hold was small and full of bales, heavy packages wrapped in layers of thick cloth interspersed with waterproof membranes. Dumarest checked the restraints then, as the engineer, bored, left him to it, slipped the knife from his boot and thrust the point deep into a bale. Withdrawing it he smelled the blade, catching the odor of dried meat seasoned with spice. Chelach meat processed for export—an unusual cargo to carry into the Hichen Cloud.

Thoughtfully he continued his examination. In one corner he found a heap of crates and with his knife levered one open. Inside lay an assortment of thick clothing, heavy boots, gauntlets with metal insets, thick metal mesh designed to protect the face and eyes. Another held the converse, light clothing suitable for a tropical climate together with curved, razor-sharp machetes. A box held stubby, automatic weapons, light machine guns together with ammunition. The rest of the crates held foods of various kinds; highly concentrated pastes, dried fruits, compotes of nuts mixed with berries, together with beads, knives, bolts of cloth, tawdry ornaments.

Trade goods for a primitive people and survival gear for a variety of climates. Weapons to crush opposition and food to maintain life. Clear evidence that Sufan Noyoka wasn't sure of what he would find if and when they reached the Ghost World.

In the salon Marek Cognez was telling fortunes. In his hands the cards rustled with a smooth deftness, falling to immediately appear on the table, their descent accelerated by the relative effects of time.

"An interesting life," he mused. "In youth you have known passion and I see traces of a great disappointment. There is pain and, yes, an eroding despair. Yet there is hope." His finger touched a card. "Not great but present. Diminish the influence of the Lord of Fools and it will gain in dominance."

"Which tells me nothing," said Usan Labria sourly. "Is this your trade, Marek, to gull idiots at a fair?"

"My trade?" He smiled and gathered the cards, quickly dealing two hands, both good, one, his own, better than the other. "A man makes his way as best he can and who then can speak of trades? Let us say that I have a small ability, an attribute or a talent if you prefer to call it that. Give me the parts of a pattern and I will read you the whole."

"Like a cyber?" said Pacula.

"No. A servant of the Cyclan works on a basis of extrapolated logic. From two facts he will build three, five, a dozen. Give him a situation and, for each proposed change, he will predict the most probable sequence of events. I work on intuition."

"But you both tell fortunes," said Usan. Her tone was contemptuous.

"No. I do not deal with the future." Marek shuffled and dealt and studied the cards. "Last night you dreamed of youth," he said. "Of firm young arms around you, of warm lips against your own. Am I wrong?"

The question shook her with its sudden demand, so that she sat, a dull tinge mottling her sunken cheeks, the hands clenching as they rested on the table.

Dumarest said quietly, "To be clever is one thing, Marek. To insult is another."

"So you spring to her defense?" The man's eyes were sharp, the interest masked by a smile. "An old woman and a fighter. Often the two are found together but this time, I think, not for the usual reason. And you, Pacula, did you also dream?"

This time it was her turn to flush and she glared at the man, hating him, wishing him dead.

"Marek, you go too far," said Jarv Nonach. "One day your humor will kill you."

The navigator sat slumped in a chair, a pomander in his hand which he lifted at intervals to his thin, hooked nose. His cheeks, blotched with scabrous tissue, were puffed, his eyes mere slits beneath swollen brows, the neck bulging over the collar of his uniform. The pomander was of a delicate filigree, the container filled with the aromatic drugs to which he had become addicted. A man who spoke seldom and who, when not on duty, spent long hours sunk into a mental stupor—a condition which seemed to banish his need for sleep.

Shrugging, Marek said, "To die with a smile is surely the best way to go. Earl, you agree?"

"Why ask when you claim to know the answer?"

"Each man holds within himself the absolute truth, yet that truth may not be in tune with that of others. Have you ever thought of that? Or are you too engrossed in small needs to open your mind to a greater universe? Tell me, Earl, when you fight and when you kill, is it only then you feel truly alive? There is a name for such men—shall I tell you what it is?"

A man weary of life, thought Pacula, one tempting destruction. Then, looking at Dumarest, she knew he was wasting his time. No insult could spur that man to action if he was conscious of a greater need. Later, perhaps, he would take his revenge, but not now and, she guessed, Marek must know it. Then why the gibes and sneers, the invitation to combat?

A weakness, she decided. A desire to prove himself or the pleasure he gained in risking danger as another would deliberately walk on the edge of a precipice for no good reason, tempting fate for a perverse amusement. The price he paid for his talent, though as yet she had seen nothing of it.

As if reading her thoughts he said, "You play chess, Pacula? Set up the board, arrange the men how you will, take any side, and in twelve moves I will beat you. Or give me a string of numbers and ask for any result, division, multiplication, the square roots, anything. The stanza of a poem—one you know—give me the first half and I will give you the second, and if I am at fault, it is the poet who will be wrong, not I."

"Games," said Usan. "How can they help us?"

"Who knows what we may find?" Marek dropped the cards, and no longer mocking, looked from one to the other. "A safe the combination of which is unknown? A situation we cannot recognize? A world of mystery in which only special talents can find a path? Sufan has an artifact—have you seen it? A mass of distorted metal found on a wrecked vessel. A scrap of debris, some would think, but I can fit it into a pattern. As I helped to fit other items into a whole. You think he guides you to Balhadorha?" His finger thrust at where Jarv Nonach sat sniffing his pomander. "He takes us only where it is determined we should go."

"On a route you have plotted?" Usan Labria stared her disbelief. "To the Ghost World?"

"No, to Chamelard. First to Chamelard." Marek scooped up the cards. "And now, Earl, shall we play?"

Sufan Noyoka sat in his cabin, the desk before him heaped with papers, graphs bright with colored lines. He looked up as Dumarest entered the room, saying nothing as the door closed, only his eyes moving, darting from one point to another as if he were an animal trapped in a cage.

Dumarest said flatly, "It is time we talked."

"More than time, Earl, I agree, but I have been busy, as you know, and you have had your own duties. You have assessed the crew?"

"Men united by greed."

"True," admitted Sufan, "but how else to pursuade men to risk their lives? The danger will come when their determination begins to fail. Then they must be urged to continue the search. And when we find Balhadorha there will be other dangers." He touched a paper, moved a graph, rested his hand on a star map. "You remember the artifact I showed you? Once it was the part of a machine, probably the power supply, and it could have been of incredible value. Those on the wrecked vessel must have found it and then what? Did each try to gain it for his own? Greed knows no bounds, Earl—a danger I early recognized. And what can two women and an old man do against the rest?"

"You forget Marek."

"Who could instigate the trouble. What do you think of him?"

"I think he is a man in love with death," said Dumarest. "Only when dead will he know the final mystery of life. Where did you find him?"

"Does it matter? I needed him and so he is with us. As I needed you, Earl. The reason must be obvious."

A part, but not the whole. Men faced with sudden wealth could become intoxicated at a prospect of fortune and forget elementary precautions. A fact Dumarest had recognized, but he sensed there must be more.

"Why are we calling at Chamelard?"

"You know?"

"Marek announced it."

"Well, it is no secret." Sufan shrugged, a gesture which minimized the importance of the event. "I would have told you long before we landed. An essential part of the plan, Earl. Our number is not yet complete. There is another we have to collect."

"A man?"

"A woman."

"And the cargo of Chelach meat?"

"To buy her."

Sufan rose and stepped to where a container filled with a murky liquid stood on a small table beside the cot. Touching its base, he activated the device and watched as a pale luminescence grew within, swirls of color which gained strength to take on a vaguely amorphous shape, delicate membranes moving with slow grace in a sea of divergent hues.

Without turning he said, "To buy her, Earl. Money would

have been simpler but my funds are exhausted. My herd, too, now that I have turned it into meat. Unless we find Balhadorha I am ruined."

A doubt, the first he had expressed, and Dumarest was conscious of the man's tension, the strain barely controlled, masked by his apparent interest in the luminous toy. As it glowed still brighter Dumarest leaned forward and switched it off. Even though never still the man's eyes could reveal hidden intent.

"Is Chamelard a slave world?"

"No, but the woman is special, a product of the Schell-Peng Laboratories. She has been trained, her special attributes strengthened, skills honed and developed to a high degree over the years. We need her if we are to navigate the Hichen Cloud."

Then, as Dumarest made no comment, he said, "The essence of my plan, Earl. If a few men and a ship could find Balhadorha, then why hasn't it been discovered before? The area around the Hichen Cloud is thick with worlds and traders are always on the search for a profit. Given time, it would have been found; instead it remains a legend. Why? A question I pondered for years and then had what must be the answer. Balhadorha is within the Cloud and the entire region is a mass of conflicting energies. In it normal instruments are distorted and true navigation impossible. You have been close to such regions, Earl, you know what happens."

Sensors at fault, readings turned into meaningless information, a ship twisted and torn, helpless to aim for safety, not knowing even where safety could be found. The generator would be overstrained, units fail, the Erhaft Field collapse. Once that happened, unless the vessel was crushed like an egg, it would drift helpless in a sea of destructive radiation.

Something the crew members would have known, and Dumarest wondered at their silence. Or perhaps, even now, they were ignorant of the true extent of the danger.

He said, "Does the captain know you intend to penetrate the Cloud?"

"Rae Acilus has my confidence."

"And the others? Do they think, as I did, that you merely intended to skirt the edges?"

"Does it matter?" Sufan was bland. "They have come too far to back out now."

A mistake—when the trouble began they would lose their

hunger for riches, the need to survive would see to that. Then he remembered Usan Labria and her determination. She had nothing to lose. Neither did Pacula, who would take any chance to find her daughter. Marek? He would welcome the challenge.

It was enough to worry about himself. Once on Chamelard the expedition could go to hell without him.

Chapter 8

It was a cold world, a frigid ball of ice circling a dying sun, the ruby light from the primary doing little more than to paint the snow and frost with deceptively warm radiance. The town was small, the houses huddled close, the field deserted aside from the *Mayna.* The few men in attendance were shapeless in thick garments, a rime of frost over the fabric covering their mouths.

A planet strange to Dumarest, but he knew at once it was not one on which to be stranded. And there were other complications: a man who stood watching without apparent reason as he and Sufan Noyoka left the vessel, another who followed, a third who moved quickly from the gate as if to relay a message.

Small things, but his life rested on trifles, the ability to spot as unusual pattern, to sense the presence of danger.

And a cyber had landed on Teralde.

The knowledge was a prickle which stimulated him to continual awareness. Dumarest never made the mistake of underestimating the Cyclan and knew too well the subtle ways in which the organization moved. The cyber could have learned from Avorot of his presence on Teralde. He would have searched, found nothing, used the power of his mind to determine the obvious. Sufan Noyoka had an association with Chamelard, and if the cyber had learned of it, already the Cyclan could be poised ready to strike.

The Schell-Peng Laboratories rested a mile from town, a long, low, rambling structure, the walls unbroken, the roof steeply pitched. Inside it was warm with generated heat, the receptionist waiting as they opened the thick clothing they had worn for the journey.

"Sufan Noyoka? A moment." He turned to a file and busied himself with the contents. "A woman, you say?"

"Number XV2537. There was a special arrangement."

"Which would place it in the special file." The man moved to another cabinet. A purposeful delay or merely an accustomed lethargy? Dumarest turned and studied the area with apparent casualness. Aside from the receptionist they were alone in the chamber except for a man engrossed in a book. A strange place in which to read if he were not waiting the result of an inquiry.

"Sir?" The receptionist looked up from the file. "The subject in question is not available at this time."

"Why not?"

"A matter of payment. Two installments have been missed and—"

"A lie!"

"Perhaps. An investigation will clear the matter. In the meantime she is being held in storage." The man came to the counter, smiling. "A small delay, sir, no more. The records will have to be checked and the discrepancy isolated."

Dumarest said, "How much does he owe?"

"The installments came to—"

"The total?"

"The sum for outright purchase is ten thousand elmars. That, naturally, includes the installments and full compensation for storage and revival."

It was too much. Dumarest knew it before Sufan Noyoka protested.

"Our agreement was for five thousand. My cargo has been sold for four and a half and I have the rest in cash. I demand that you hold to our agreement."

"But, of course, sir. The reputation of the Schell-Peng is well-known and all contracts will be honored. It is just a matter of the records. Once we have made an investigation I'm sure that all will be well. A matter of a few days. I will make a special clearance-order on the query."

"I want the woman now!"

"That is impossible. Of course, if you have the full amount? No? Then, reluctantly, I must insist you exercise patience. A few days, sir."

Dumarest's hand clamped on Sufan's arm as he was about to object. Quietly he said, "A few days? Well, at least it will give us a chance to see the sights. What do you recommend?"

"The Signal Mount is very good at this time of year. I think you will enjoy it. And if you have a mind to ski the Frendish Slopes are ideal."

"And a place to stay? Never mind," said Dumarest before the man could answer. "We'll find something. In three days, then?"

"Yes, sir. That will be fine. Three days and all will be ready."

As they left, Dumarest glanced at the man reading the book. He was a slow reader. Not once had he turned a page.

At night Chamelard turned into a frozen hell, the air crackling with cold, the thin wind which blew from the open stretches touching with the burn of knives. Above, the stars burned with a cold ferocity, seeming to suck the warmth from living flesh, the sprawling mass of the Hichen Cloud a malignant eye.

Hunched in his clothing Marek beat his gloved hands together, his voice a husky complaint.

"Earl, this is madness. Why don't we just wait?"

Something Dumarest dared not do. A night had passed, a day, and now on the second night time was running out. Already he had waited too long, but Marek had needed to make inquiries as to the laboratory, assembling the parts of a puzzle which he, with his talent, had built into a whole.

The structure and layout of the buildings. The probable paths any guards would take, the routine followed by the staff, the strength of any opposition.

A gamble on which Dumarest was staking his life.

To wait on Chamelard was to be taken by the Cyclan. The *Mayna* was the only means by which he could leave—and Sufan would not go without the mysterious woman. To steal her was the only answer.

Behind them Timus Omilcar swore as he slipped to fall heavily, rolling on the frost-hardened ground. The pack of extra clothing on his back gave him the appearance of an ungainly beast. As he rose his voice was an angry mutter.

"How much further? Damn this cold! How can men survive such weather?"

Few did and less tried. The streets were deserted, each house firmly shuttered, the two illuminated only by starlight. Ahead reared the bulk of the laboratories, walls of blank stone rising to the eaves of the pitched roof, the doors sealed. No guards were visible and none were needed. No ordinary thief could use what the laboratory contained.

"Wait!" Marek paused as they reached the nearest corner. "Let me orient myself." He turned, a thin plume of vapor streaming from his mask, then grunted and stepped forward. The wall dropped, rose, swung to the right. Beyond a narrow extension which left the main structure like a wing lay a circular expanse. "Here!"

"Are you sure?" The engineer lurched forward. "It looks all the same to me."

Dumarest said nothing. If a mistake had been made then all would be lost, but he had to trust the man's abilities. His neck, also, would be at risk.

"If the woman is in storage she'll be beyond that wall," insisted Marek. "And if we don't get on with it and soon we might as well join her. My hands are numb. Earl?"

"Up," said Dumarest. "Against the wall, Timus."

He climbed the man's shoulders, standing facing the wall as Marek swarmed up the living ladder, to grip the eave and to pull himself onto the roof. Dumarest gripped the rope he lowered, climbed it, hauled the engineer up after him. Together, crouching against the wind, they moved over the slabbed tiles, halting at Marek's signal.

"Here," he muttered. "And for God's sake hurry. This wind is killing me."

From a pack Dumarest took a laser and held it close as the beam ate through the stone. Little flecks of molten rock, caught by the wind, rose to burn like dying stars. Wedging his knife into the burned slot Dumarest completed the circle and levered up the freed portion. Below lay thick insulation, beyond it a gap faced with sheets of plastic. Penetrating it they were through and into the building.

The roof was a dozen feet above the floor of a chamber illuminated by a soft, blue light. In it a double row of caskets ran along facing walls. One end of the room was blank, the other pierced by a wide door, now closed. No guards were in attendance.

"Earl?" Timus's voice was a whisper.

"It's safe."

Dumarest swung himself through the opening and dropped lightly to the floor. As the others joined him he handed the laser to the engineer, gestured, and as the man went to weld fast the door, moved quickly along the rows of caskets. Most were empty, those with occupants sealed, each container emblazoned with a number.

"Here!" called Marek softly. "XV2537. Right?"

The number Sufan had given and the receptionist had not

lied. Through the transparent lid Dumarest could see a female shape, details blurred by a film of frost. Carefully he checked the installation, taking the time despite the need for haste. The chamber could be monitored and, at any moment a guard could check the scanner. Even their own body heat, raising the temperature in the vicinity of the casket, could trigger an alarm.

"Can you manage it, Earl?" The door welded, the engineer had come to stand at his side.

"Yes." The equipment was sophisticated and better than that found on ships, but that was to be expected. It was meant to handle men, not beasts, and valuable property needed to be treated with care. "Drag some of those empty caskets under the hole so we can climb to the roof. Marek, stand by the door and signal if you hear anyone approach."

As they ran to obey Dumarest activated the mechanism and set the reviving cycle into motion.

At first nothing could be seen aside from the flash of a signal lamp telling of invisible energies at work. Within the casket eddy currents warmed the frigid body, penetrating skin and flesh and bone to heat it uniformly throughout. Then the heart stimulator, the pulmotor to activate the lungs, the drugs to numb the pain of returning circulation. Without them she would scream her lungs raw with agony.

Minutes which dragged but could not be hastened.

"Earl!" Marek called from his position at the door. "Someone's coming."

A routine check or a guard investigating an alarm? Either made no difference, when the door refused to open he would summon others. It jarred as if to a blow, jarred again, the metallic clanging sounding oddly loud in the silence of the chamber.

"That's it!" Timus sucked in his breath and looked at the hole in the roof. "They've found us. Do we make a run for it, Earl?"

"No. Get that spare clothing ready."

Naked, the woman would have to be protected against the external cold. As the door jarred to a renewed impact Dumarest stared at the casket, mentally counting seconds. Soon now. It had to be soon.

The lid hissed open as the door bulged inward.

"Get her out, dressed, and up to the roof," snapped Dumarest. "Timus, give me the laser."

He ran back to the door as the others set to work, using the beam to set new welds, fusing metal into a composite whole in a dozen places around the panel. He ducked as heat seared his face, the beam of an external laser turning the metal red, sending molten droplets falling like rain.

Within seconds they would have burned a hole in the panel exposing the chamber to their fire. Stepping back, Dumarest aimed and triggered the laser, sending the beam through the opening, hearing a cry of pain, a man's savage curse.

"My arm!"

"Stand aside, fool!"

A momentary delay during which another would have to pick up the fallen laser and get it into operation. Dumarest turned and ran down the chamber. The others had vanished through the hole in the roof. Reaching the casket, which had been dragged beneath it, he sprang, hit the top, continued the movement upward, his hands catching the edges of the hole, lifted him up and into the space beneath the roof. As he moved on upward the beam of a laser burned the plastic an inch from the heel of his boot.

"Earl!" Timus called as Dumarest emerged from the roof into the starlight. "Which way?"

They were crouched on the steep pitch of the roof, the woman a shapeless bundle in the engineer's arms. Marek, sprawled to one side, panted like a dog, his head wreathed in pluming vapor.

"Up and over!" Dumarest pointed to the ridge. "Drop on the other side and run. Move!"

"And you?"

"I'll follow."

The guards were too close—already they must have reached the hole and within seconds would have made an appearance. Unless stopped they would have a clear target. As the others scrabbled up the slope Dumarest crouched at the edge of the opening, lying flat, his hands stiffened, the fingers held close, the palms rigid.

Tensely he waited, hearing a man's panting breath, the sound of movement, a rasp as something metallic tore at the insulation beneath the tiles. A hand appeared holding a gun, an arm followed by a head, the face pale in the starlight. As the man turned toward him Dumarest was already in motion, his left hand reaching, chopping at the wrist, the gun falling to slide clattering over the tiles as his right hand stabbed like a blunted spear at the point of the neck beneath the ear.

A blow which numbed and paralyzed, robbing the man of speech and motion so that he hung limp in the opening, blocking it against his companions.

Before they could clear the obstruction Dumarest had reached the ridge, was over it, sliding down the steep slope to the edge of the roof, hurtling over it to land heavily, rolling on the frosty ground. As a siren blasted the air he was up and running.

Ahead he saw the others, Marek running with a lithe grace, the engineer puffing, hampered by his burden.

"We'll never make it!" he said as Dumarest reached his side. "There'll be lights, guards—and we've a long way to go."

"Keep moving. Head straight for the ship and get ready to leave. Hurry!"

"But—"

"Move, damn you! Move!"

Alerted, the guards would be streaming from the building to surround the area. Their only hope lay in speed, but speed wasn't enough. Soon there would be lights, and unless they were distracted, the guards would quickly run them down. Dumarest slowed as a blaze of light came from the open door of the building, turning to run toward it, across it, away from the others. He heard a yell, a shouted command, and the ruby guide-beam of a laser reached toward him.

It missed as he dived toward a low mound, dropping behind it to run, to rise and deliberately expose himself against the stars, to drop and run again as men chased after him.

A long chase during which he led them from the others making a wending path back to town, once feeling the burn of a near miss as a laser touched the edge of his clothing, beating out the small fire with his gloved hand.

At the field two men stood at the gate, a third running toward them as Dumarest approached. Too many men to be out in such weather. Beyond them he could see the open port of the *Mayna*, Marek standing in the entrance.

"Mister?" A man stepped toward him as Dumarest neared the gate. "Just a moment. You from that ship?"

He fell, doubled and retching as Dumarest kicked him in the stomach. His companion, reaching for something in his pocket, followed as a stiffened hand slashed at his throat. The third man, halting, backed, lifting something which gleamed in the starlight.

"You there! Move and I'll burn you!"

He was too far to be reached and to run was to be crippled, at least. Then, from where he stood in the open port, Marek screamed.

It was a sound startling in its sheer unexpectedness. A raw, wordless shriek as if from a stricken beast, and instinctively, the armed man turned toward it, the gun lifting against the threat. A moment of inattention, but it was enough. Before he could realize his error Dumarest was on him, ducking low as the weapon fired, rising to knock it aside with a sweep of his left hand, the clenched fist of the right driving into the fabric covering the mouth, feeling bone yield as the man went down.

"Earl!" shouted Marek. "More are coming. Hurry!"

Dumarest ran toward the ship, hearing shouts from behind, the roar of aimed weapons. Against lasers he would have stood no chance, but they were armed with missile throwers, and dodging, he made a poor target. A bullet kicked dirt close to his foot, another hummed like a bee past his ear, a third slammed against the bull.

Then, as he passed through the port, a bullet struck the edge of the opening, whined with a vicious ricochet to slam against his temple and send him falling into a bottomless pit of darkness.

Chapter 9

He woke to find Usan Labria at his side. She said, "How do you feel, Earl?"

"Your turn to ask the questions?"

"That's right. And my turn to look after you. Well?"

Dumarest stretched. He lay on his cot, nude but for shorts, and beneath the fingers he rested on the bulkhead he could feel the unmistakable vibration of the Erhaft Field. He felt well aside from a ravenous hunger and could guess the reason.

"Slow-time?"

"Yes." The woman held a steaming cup and handed it to him. "I guess you could use this."

It was the basic food of spacemen, a liquid sickly with glucose, heavy with protein, laced with vitamins. A measure would provide nourishment for a day. A unit in the base of the container kept it warm.

As he drank she said, "You were lucky. A fraction to the left and the bullet would have spattered your brains. As it was you had a torn scalp and a minor fracture."

"Then why the slow-time?"

"Why not? There's no point in suffering if you don't have to. I made Sufan provide it a day after we left. You've been under five hours, close to seven days subjective."

Eight days total in which his body had healed, seven of them due to the acceleration of his metabolism provided by the drug. The reverse of quick-time. Dumarest sat upright, touching his temple, feeling nothing but the scab of the newly healed wound. One eight days old, the injury mending while he had lain in drugged unconsciousness.

"Still hungry?" Usan Labria had a second cup. She handed it to him, talking while he drank, this time more slowly. "Acilus left as soon as the port was sealed. Sufan insisted and I think he was right. Those men intended to get you."

72

"Guards from the Schell-Peng."

"No." She was positive. "They weren't from the laboratory. Those that came later, maybe, but not the ones waiting at the gate. They didn't try to stop the others and had no interest in the girl. They were after you, Earl, and I think you knew it. The question is, why?"

She was too shrewd and a woman with her desperation posed a perpetual danger. Once she even guessed he could provide what she needed how could he trust her?

"You're guessing," he said. "But if you find the answer let me know."

"So it's none of my business. Is that it?" She shrugged. "Well, have it your own way."

Setting down the empty cup Dumarest rose, breathing deeply, expanding his chest so that the thin tracery of scars on his torso shone livid in the light. He felt a momentary weakness, the result of days of inactivity as his hunger was the result of days of starvation.

"I didn't bother to give you intravenous feeding," said Usan. "A man like you can afford to starve for a while." Her eyes roved his body, lingering on the scars. "A fighter," she mused. "I'd guessed as much. Naked blades in the ring to first-blood or death. And you learned the hard way."

Young, inexperienced, earning money in the only way he could. Saving his life by natural speed, taking wounds, killing to the roar of a mob. Bearing now the signs of his tuition.

Dressed, he said, "Where is the girl?"

"In the cabin next to Sufan's. She was in a bad way when Timus carried her in. The shock of revival coupled with exposure—for a while we thought she'd die."

"And?"

"She recovered. Sufan worked on her and Pacula acted as nurse. She's all right now." Usan hesitated, "But there's something wrong with her, Earl. She isn't normal."

"In what way?"

"She—oh, to hell with it, let Sufan explain."

He answered the door when Dumarest knocked at the cabin and stepped outside and into the corridor, speaking quickly, his voice low.

"I'm glad to see you on your feet, Earl. You had me worried for a time, that wound looked nasty and any blow on the head can give rise to complications."

"The girl?"

"Inside. You did well getting her out—but don't expect too much. Remember that her talent is extremely rare, and always, there is a price to pay for such an attribute as she possesses. She—" He broke off, his eyes darting, glinting like the scales of fish in a sunlit pool, touching Dumarest, the woman at his side, the light above, the deck, his hands. "When you see her, Earl, be gentle. It is not quite what it seems."

"What isn't?"

Then, as the man hesitated, Usan Labria said harshly, "Why don't you tell him, Sufan? Why be so delicate? Earl, the girl is blind!"

She stood against the far wall of the cabin, tall, dressed in a simple white gown caught at the waist with a cincture of gold. A dress Pacula had provided as she had tended the mane of fine, blonde hair, which gathered, hung in a shimmering tress over the rounded left shoulder. As she had painted the nails of hands and naked feet a warm crimson and bathed and scented the contours of the ripely feminine body.

A warm and lovely creature—and blind!

Dumarest saw the eyes, milky orbs of gleaming opalescence, edged with the burnish of lashes, set high and deep above prominent cheekbones. The mouth was full, the lower lip sensuous, the chin delicately pointed.

A face he had never seen before but one which held haunting traces of familiarity.

"You noticed it too," said Pacula quietly. She moved to stand beside the girl. "Usan remarked on it. She said we could almost be sisters."

"A coincidence," said Sufan Noyoka quickly. "It can be nothing else. My dear, this is Earl Dumarest. He brought you to us."

Dumarest stepped forward and took the lifted hand, holding it cupped in his own as if it were a delicate bird.

"My lady."

"She has no name," said Pacula. "Only a number."

"Then why not give her one? Cul—"

"No," she interrupted fiercely. "Not Culpea. That belongs to my daughter."

"I was going to say Culephria," said Dumarest mildly. "After a world similar to Chamelard."

"No, it is too much the same. And she cannot be Culpea, she is too old. Much too old."

A fact obvious when looking at her. The missing girl had been twelve, this woman was at least twice that age.

"We'll call her Embira," said Usan. "I once had—we'll call her Embira. Would you like that, my dear?"

"It sounds a nice name. Embira. Embira. Yes, I like it."

Her voice was soft, almost childish in its lack of emotional strength, matching the smooth, unmarked contours of her face. Dumarest watched as Pacula guided her to a chair. She sat as a child would sit, very upright, hands cradled in her lap. Her eyes, like fogged mirrors, stared directly ahead, adding to the masklike quality of her features.

Dumarest gestured Sufan Noyoka from the cabin. When the door had closed behind them he said flatly, "A blind girl—you expect her to guide us to Balhadorha?"

"Not blind, Earl, not in the way you mean. I told you she had an attribute. She can see, but not as we can. Her mind can register the presence of matter and energy far better than any instrument. She—"

"How did you know about her?"

"I have my ways. And the Schell-Peng laboratories have theirs. They took her when young and trained and developed her talent. A rare mutation or an unusual gene diversion— the results are all that matter. Enough that she is with us and already we are approaching the Hichen Cloud. Soon she will guide us. Soon, Earl, we shall reach our goal."

A statement of conviction or hope? Dumarest said, "If the girl can't do as you say, we are all heading toward destruction. How can you be certain she has the attribute you claim?"

"She has it." Sufan made a small gesture of confidence. "I trust the Schell-Peng."

"I don't." Dumarest jerked open the door of the cabin. "Pacula. Usan, please step outside. I want to talk to the girl alone."

"What do you intend?" Pacula was suspicious. "If—"

"Don't be a fool!" snapped Usan impatiently. "Earl has his reasons and he won't hurt her. Let him do as he wants. I trust him if you don't."

Alone with the girl, Dumarest stood for a moment with his back to the closed door, then stepped to where she sat.

Abruptly he moved his hand toward her eyes, halting his fingers an inch from the blank orbs.

"You almost touched me," she said evenly.

"You felt the wind?"

"That and more, Earl. I may call you that?"

"Yes, Embira, but how did you know it was me?"

His tread, perhaps, sharp ears could have distinguished it. His odor, the normally undetectable exudations from his body, recognized by a dog so why not by a girl trained to use the rest of her senses?

"Your aura," she said. "I can tell your aura. You carry metal and wear more. The others do not."

The knife he carried in his boot and the mesh buried in the plastic of his clothing. An electronic instrument could have determined as much—was she no more than that?

Stepping back from the chair Dumarest said, "I am going to move about the cabin. Tell me where I am and, if possible, what I am doing."

He moved toward the door, stepped to the right, the left, approached her and retreated and, each time, she correctly gave his movement. A small block of clear plastic stood on a table, an ornament containing an embedded flower. He picked it up, tossed it, threw it suddenly toward her.

His aim had been good, it missed her face by more than an inch, but she had made no effort to ward off the missile.

"Did you see that?"

"See?"

"Observe, sense, become aware." Baffled he sought for another word to explain sight. "Determine?"

"Krang," she said. "At the laboratory they called it krang. No, I could not krang it."

"Why not?"

"It had no aura."

Plastic and a dead flower, yet both were mass and a radar installation would have been able to track the path of the object. Too small, perhaps? A matter of density?

He said, "How many others ride this ship?"

"Seven." Frowning, she added, "I think, seven. One is hard to determine. His aura is hazed and lost at times."

The engineer, his aura diffused by the energies emitted by the generator—if she was registering raw energy. If she could see, or krang it.

Sitting on the cot Dumarest tried to understand. A mind

which could determine the presence of energy or mass if it was large or dense enough. Every living thing radiated energy, every machine, every piece of decaying matter. To be blind to the normal spectrum of light, yet to be able to "see" the varying auras of fluctuating fields, to isolate them, to state their movements against the background of other auras.

What else was normal sight? Only the terminology was different. He saw in shape and form and color, she distinguished patterns. He saw solid objects of isolated mass, she recognized force fields and stress-complexes, "auras" of varying size, hue, and form.

Sufan's guide to find a dream.

He said, "Embira, how long were you with the Schell-Peng?"

"All my life."

"As far back as you can remember, you mean. They wouldn't have taken you as a baby. Was your past never mentioned?"

"No, Earl. They trained me. Always they trained me, and sometimes they hurt me. I think they did things——" Her hands lifted toward her face, her eyes. "No. I can't remember."

It was kinder not to press. Rising, Dumarest said, "I want to examine you, Embira. I may touch you, do you mind?"

"No."

Her face turned up toward him as he lifted fingers beneath her chin, the cheeks petal-smooth, the forehead unlined. Her skin was warm with a velvet softness and the perfume Pacula had sprayed onto her hair rose to engulf him in a scented cloud. Carefully he studied her eyes, seeing no sign of scars or adapted tissue. The balls seemed to be covered with an opaque film shot with lambent strands, the irises and pupils invisible.

"Earl, your hands, they are so firm."

"I won't hurt you. Can you move your eyes? No? Never mind."

The gown had long sleeves. He lifted them and looked at the expanse of her arms.

"Do you want to see the rest of me, Earl?" Her voice was innocent of double meaning. "Shall I undress?"

"No, that won't be necessary. Do you know why you are here, Embira?"

"Sufan Noyoka told me. I am to guide you."

"Can you?"

"I don't know, Earl, but I will try. I will do anything you want."

"No, Embira," he said, harshly. "Not what I want. Not what Sufan Noyoka wants or any other person. You're not a slave. You do as you want and nothing else. You understand?"

"But I was bought—"

"You were stolen," he interrupted. "You belong to no one but yourself. You owe nothing to anyone."

A lesson he tried to drive home. The girl was too vulnerable and had yet to be armored against the cruel reality of life.

For a long moment she sat, silent, then said, slowly, "You mean well, Earl, I know that. But you are wrong. I do owe you something. But only you, Earl. For you I would do anything."

A child speaking with an unthinking innocence, unaware of the implication, the unspoken invitation. Then, looking at her, he realized how wrong that was. She was not a child but a fully mature woman with all a woman's instincts. His touch had triggered a response to his masculinty; a biochemical reaction as old as time.

Aware of his scrutiny she said, "At the laboratories they told me I was very beautiful. Am I?"

"Yes."

"And you like me?"

"You're a member of this expedition. I like you no more and no less than the others."

Outside the cabin Pacula was waiting, Marek at her side. As she brushed past Dumarest and closed the door he smiled.

"The girl has stimulated her maternal instincts, Earl. Twice I had to stop her from interfering. And, of course, there could be a touch of jealously. The girl is very lovely, don't you agree?"

Dumarest said, "I owe you thanks."

"For the scream? It was nothing, a diversion created without personal danger, and it amused me to see you overcome those men." Pausing, Marek added casually, "One other thing, Earl. It might interest you to know we are being followed."

"A ship?"

"From Chamelard. It left shortly after we did, but don't

worry, we are pulling ahead. And contact is impossible. A small accident to the radio, you understand. I thought it wise."

How much did the man know or suspect? A lover of puzzles, a man proud of his talent, could he have associations with the Cyclan? And Dumarest could guess what the following ship contained. A cyber who had predicted his movements and had arrived on Chamelard a little too late.

He said, "The Schell-Peng must be eager for revenge."

"That's what I thought." Marek's eyes were bland. "And with a captain like ours it would be stupid to take chances. He would think nothing of cooperating if the reward were high enough. Us evicted, the girl handed over, money received, the *Mayna* his without question—why should he risk his neck searching for a legendary world?"

A facile explanation and, Dumarest hoped, a true one. But from a man who courted danger?

A matter of degree, he decided. The risk of betrayal was nothing against the perils that waited for them in the Hichen Cloud.

Chapter 10

The first shock came ten days later, a jerk as if the vessel had been struck by a giant hand, and as the alarms shrilled Dumarest ran to the control room. The girl was already at her station, sitting in a chair behind the one occupied by Rae Acilus.

The captain was curt. "There is no place for you here, Earl."

"I want him to stay." Embira reached out and took his hand, groping until he placed his fingers within her own. "Earl, you stay with me?"

"I'll stay."

"Then don't interfere." Acilus's voice was the rap of a martinet. "I've enough to think about as it is. Jarv?"

The navigator was at his post, Sufan Noyoka at his side. On all sides massed instruments hummed and flashed in quiet efficiency; electronic probes and sensors scanning the void, a computer correlating the assembled information, mechanical brains, eyes and fingers which alone could guide the vessel on its path from star to star.

Again the ship jerked, warning bells ringing, the alarms dying as the captain hit a switch. An impatient gesture born of necessity—within the Cloud the alarms would be constant.

Dumarest stared at the picture depicted on the screens.

He had been in dust clouds before, riding traders risking destruction for the sake of profit, and had no illusions as to the dangers they faced. The space ahead, filled with broken atoms and minute particles of matter was an electronic maelstrom. Opposed charges, building, wrenched the very fabric of the continuum and altered the normal laws of space and time. Only by delicate questing and following relatively safe paths could a vessel hope to survive and always was the danger of shifting nodes of elemental force, which could turn a ship into molten ruin, rip it, turn it inside out, crush it so as to leave the crew little more than crimson smears.

And the *Mayna* was going too fast. Sufan had placed too much faith in the girl's ability.

"Up!" she said. "Quickly!"

Ahead space looked normal, the instruments registering nothing but a dense magnetic field, but the forces which affected the registers could affect human brains so eyes saw other than reality.

"Obey!" snapped Sufan as the captain hesitated. "Follow Embira's instructions at all times without hesitation."

The ship sang as, too late, the captain moved his controls. A thin, high-pitched ringing which climbed to the upper limit of audibility and beyond. Dumarest felt the pain at his ears, saw ruby glitters sparkle from the telltales, then it was over as they brushed the edge of the danger.

Opposing currents which had vibrated the hull as if it had been a membrane shaken by a wind. Yet, around them, space seemed clear.

"Left," she said and then quickly, "and down!"

This time Acilus obeyed without delay.

Dumarest said, "What route are we following?"

As yet Sufan had been mysterious, conferring with Jarv Nonach and Marek Cognez alone, making computations and avoiding questions. Hugging the secret of his discovery as if it were a precious gem. But now Dumarest wanted answers.

"Tell me, Sufan. How do we find Balhadorha?"

"We must reach the heart of the Cloud," said the man reluctantly. "There are three suns in close proximity and the Ghost World should be at the common point between them."

"Should be?"

"Will be?" Sufan blazed his impatience. "For years I have devoted my life to this matter. Trust me, Earl. I know what I'm doing." He stared at the paper in his hand, muttering to the navigator, then said, "Captain, you are off course. The correct path lies fifteen degrees to the left and three upward. There will be a star. Approach it to within fifteen units then take course. . . ."

Dumarest glanced at the girl as the man rattled a stream of figures. She was sitting, tense, her blind eyes gleaming in the subdued lighting. Her fingers, gripping his own, were tight.

"Earl?"

"I'm here, Embira. You know that. You can feel my hand."

"Your hand!" She lifted it to her cheek and held it hard against the warm velvet of her skin. "It's hard to krang you, Earl. The auras are so bright and there are so many of them. Hold me! Never let me go!"

A woman afraid and with good reason. For her normal matter did not exist, it was an obstruction, unseen, known only by touch. Instead there was a mass of lambent glows and, perhaps, shifting colors. Now she sat naked among them, conscious of lethal forces all around, denied even the comfort of the solid appearance of the protective hull. The metal, to her, would be a haze shot with streamers of prob- ing energy, startling, hurting, the cause of fear and terror.

"The left!" she said abruptly. "No, the right, quickly. Quickly. Now up! Up!"

Her voice held confusion, one which grew as the hours dragged past and, beneath his hand, Dumarest could feel her mounting tension.

He said, "The girl must have rest."

Acilus turned, snarling, "Earl, damn you, I warned you not to interfere!"

"This is madness. The instruments are confused and we're practically traveling blind."

"The girl—"

"Is only human and can think only at human speed. She's tired and has no chance to assess what she discovers. We're deep in the Cloud now. Slow down and give her a chance to rest."

"And if I don't?"

"It's my life as well as yours, Captain." Dumarest met the hooded eyes, saw the hands clench into fists as they left the controls. "Maintain control!" he rapped. "Acilus, you fool!"

Embira screamed "Turn! Turn to the right! Turn!"

Again no danger was visible or registered in the massed in- struments but as the ship obeyed the delayed action of the captain, telltales blazed in a ruby glow, the vessel itself seem- ing to change, to become a profusion of crystalline facets, familiar objects distorted by the energies affecting the sensory apparatus of the brain. A time in which they had only the guide of the girl's voice calling directions.

One in which the air shook to the sudden screaming roar

from the engine room, Timus's voice yelling over the intercom.

"The generator! It's going!"

"Cut it!" shouted Dumarest. "Cut it!"

The ship jarred as the order was obeyed, the normal appearance returning as the field died. Slumped in her chair the girl shuddered, her free hand groping, tears streaming down her cheeks.

"The pain," she whispered. "Earl, the pain!"

"It's all right," he soothed. "It's over."

"Earl!"

He pressed her hands, soothing with his presence, his face grim as he looked at the screens. The field was down, they were drifting in the Cloud and, if the generator was ruined, they were as good as dead.

Marek sat in the salon, outwardly calm, only the slight tremor of his hands as he toyed with a deck of cards revealing his inner tension.

"So we gamble, Earl, hoping that we escape danger while we drift." He turned a card and pursed his lips. "The captain is not happy."

"To hell with him."

"You abrogated his command. He would not have cut the generator."

"He forgot what he was doing. He let anger overcome him."

"True, but Rae Acilus is a hard man, Earl, and he will not forget the slight. You shamed him before others. If the opportunity rises I suggest that you kill him before he kills you." He added meaningfully, "There are others who can run the ship."

"Such as?"

"You, perhaps, my friend. And Nonach has some ability." He turned another card. "And I am not without talent."

A possibility and Dumarest considered it. One successful flight would be enough—and no captain was immortal. Others had taken over command before, need replacing trained skill. As long as they could land and walk away from the wreck it would be enough.

But first, the ship had to be repaired.

Pacula looked up from where she sat at the side of the cot as Dumarest looked into Embira's cabin. The girl was asleep, twitching restlessly, one hand clenched, the other groping. He touched it and immediately she quieted.

"She's overstrained," said Pacula accusingly. "What did you do to her in the control room?"

"Nothing."

"But—"

"She was performing her part," he interrupted curtly. "This isn't a picnic, Pacula. And she isn't made of glass to be protected. We need her talent if we hope to survive. How is Usan?"

The woman had suffered another attack and lay now on her cot. Like the girl she was asleep, but her rest was due to drugs and exhaustion. Dumarest stooped over her, touched the prominent veins in her throat, felt the clammy texture of her skin.

Pacula said, "Is she dying?"

"We are all dying."

"Don't play with words, Earl." She was irritable, annoyed at having been taken from her charge. "Will she recover?"

Already she was living on borrowed time, but her will to live dominated the weakness of her body.

Dumarest said, "Drug her. Keep her unconscious. Worry will increase the strain she is under and—"

"If we're all to die she needn't know it." Pacula was blunt. "Is that it, Earl? Your brand of mercy?"

"You have a better?"

She looked into his eyes and saw what they held, the acceptance of the harsh universe in which he lived, one against which she had been protected all her life. Who was she to condemn or judge?

"You think a lot of Usan, Earl. Why? Does she remind you of your grandmother? Your mother?"

"I remember neither."

"She saved your life with her lies. Is that it?" And then, as he made no answer, she said bleakly, "Well, now it's up to you to save hers."

"Not me," he said. "Timus Omilcar."

The engineer was hard at work. Stripped to the waist he had head and shoulders plunged into the exposed interior of the generator. As Dumarest entered the engine room he straightened, rubbing a hand over his face, his fingers leaving thick, black smears.

"Well?"

"It could be worse." Timus stretched, easing his back. "You gave the order just in time. A few more seconds and the entire generator would be rubbish. As it is we're lucky. Two units gone but we saved the rest."

Good news, but the main question had yet to be answered. Dumarest stepped to where wine rested in a rack on the bench, poured a glass, handed it to the engineer. As the man drank he said, "Can it be repaired?"

"Given time, yes. We carry spares. Have we time?"

"We're drifting, but you know that. The girl's asleep, so there could be danger we know nothing about and could do nothing to avoid if we did. As it is space seems clear and we're safe."

"For how long?"

Dumarest shrugged. Your guess is as good as mine. An hour. A day. Who can tell?"

Timus finished his wine and reached for the bottle. Dumarest made no objection, the man was fatigued, he would burn the alcohol for fuel.

"A hell of a way to end, Earl. Waiting for something to smash you to a pulp or smear you like a bug on a wall. At least that would be fast. I saw a man once, in a hospital on Jamhar. The sole survivor of a ship which had been caught in a space storm. Their field had collapsed and the vessel wrecked, but he'd been in the hold and was found." He drank half the wine. "He wasn't human, Earl. One arm was like a claw and his head looked like a rotten melon. They kept him alive with machines and ran endless tests. Wild tissue and degenerate cells, they said. The basic protoplasmic pattern distorted by radiation. They should have let him die."

"So?"

"It could already have happened to us, Earl. We could end as monsters."

"Maybe, but we aren't dead yet so why worry about it?" Dumarest filled an empty glass and lifted it in a toast. "To life, Timus. Don't give it up before you have to."

"No." The engineer drew a deep breath. "I guess I'm just tired. Well, to hell with it. I knew the risks when I joined up with this expedition."

The man had relaxed long enough. Dumarest said, "How long will it take to repair the generator?"

"Days, Earl. A week at least. It isn't enough just to replace the units. The generator has to be cleaned, checked, the new parts tuned—say six days not counting sleep."

"And if I help?"

"Six days, Earl. I assumed you would be." Timus added bleakly, "It's too long. We can't push our luck that far. It's a bust, Earl. We haven't the time."

But they could get it. Drugs would delay the need for sleep and slow-time would stretch minutes into hours. Timus blinked as Dumarest mentioned it.

"Now why the hell didn't I think of that? Slow-time. You have it?"

"Sufan has. You've used it before? No? Well just remember to be careful. You'll be touching things at forty times the normal speed and what you imagine to be a tap will be a blow which could shatter your hand. And keep eating. I'll lay on a supply of basic and Marek can deliver more. Get things ready—and no more wine."

"No wine." The engineer swallowed what was left in his glass then said meaningfully, "How long, Earl?"

"For what?"

"You know what I'm getting at. How long are we going to look for Balhadorha? Sufan's crazy and will keep us at it until we rot. I'm willing to take a chance but there has to be a limit. If it hadn't been for you we'd be as good as dead now. A thing like that alters a man's thinking. Money's fine, yes, but what good is a fortune to a dead man?"

If a fortune was to be found at all. If the Ghost World existed. If the whole adventure was something more than a crazed dream born and nurtured over the years, fed by a feverish imagination.

"We've come too far to turn back now," said Dumarest. "We'll keep looking. We'll go to where Sufan swears the Ghost World is to be found."

"And if it isn't?"

"Then we'll keep going."

To the far side of the Hichen Cloud, to a new world where he wouldn't be expected, to lose himself before the Cyclan could again pick up his trail.

"Up!" said Embira. "Up!" And then, almost immediately, "To the left! The left!"

She sat like a coiled spring, muscles rigid beneath the soft velvet of her skin, hands clenched, blind eyes wide so that they seemed about to start from their sockets. Thin lines of fatigue marred the smooth contours of her features and her hair, in disarray, hung like a tarnished skein of gold.

Standing beside her Dumarest felt the ache and burn of overstrained muscles, the dull protest of nerve and sinew. Days had passed since the repair and he had slept little since the period of concentrated effort. Timus was in little better condition, but he had rested while Dumarest had attended the girl. She had refused to work without him at her side.

"Left!" she said again. "Left!"

Ahead space blazed with a sudden release of energy, a sear of expanding forces which caused the instruments to chatter and the telltales to burn red. Another danger averted by her quick recognition, but always there were more and how long could they continue to escape?

Without turning Rae Acilus said, "We're almost at the heart of the Cloud. There are five suns—which are the three?"

Crouched beside the navigator Sufan Noyoka studied his paper and conferred with Jarv Nonach. Their voices were low, dull in the confines of the control room. The air held a heavy taint compounded of sweat and fear, their faces, in the dull lighting, peaked and drawn.

"Those set closest, Captain. They are in a triangle set on an even plane. Head for the common point."

An instruction repeated, more for the sake of self-conviction than anything else. And yet the captain wasn't to be blamed. During the nightmare journey all sense of orientation had been lost as the ship, like a questing mote, had weaved its way on a tortuous path.

"Right!" said Embira. "Down! Up again!"

Directions sharpened by her fear, but for how long would she be able to retain the fine edge of judgment without which they had no chance? Dumarest dropped his hand to her shoulder, pressed gently on the warm flesh. Beneath his fingers she relaxed a little.

"Can you krang the planet, Embira? Is there anything there?"

"No. I—yes. Earl! I can't be sure!"

Another problem to add to the rest. A planet had mass and should have stood out like a beacon to her talent, but the suns were close and could have distorted her judgment.

"There could be nothing," said the captain. "If there isn't—"

"There is! There has to be!" Sufan would admit of no possibility of failure. Search, Captain! Get to the common point and look!"

The suns were monstrous, tremendous solar furnaces glowing with radiated energy, one somberly red, one a vibrant orange, the other burning with an eye-searing violet. Acilus guided the vessel between them, his hands deft on the controls, sensing more by instinct than anything else the path of greatest safety.

"Jarv?"

"Nothing." The navigator checked his instruments. "No register."

"There has to be! Balhadorha is there, I know it! Look again!" Sufan's voice rose even higher, to tremble on the edge of hysteria. "I can't be wrong! Years of study—look again!"

A moment as the navigator adjusted his scanners and then, "Yes! Something there!" His voice fell. "No. It's gone again."

The Ghost World living up to its reputation, sometimes spotted, more often not. But instruments could be unreliable and forces other than the gravity of a planet could have affected the sensors.

Dumarest said quietly, "Embira, we're relying on you. Be calm now. Try to eliminate all auras other than those in the common point."

"Earl—I can't!"

"Try, girl! Try!"

For a moment she sat, strained and silent, then said, "Down a little. Down and to the right. No, too far. Up. Up—now straight ahead."

The screens showed nothing, but that was to be expected, the world was too distant—if what she saw was a world. And the scanners reported nothing.

"Only empty space," said Jarv bleakly. "Some radiation flux and an intense magnetic field, but that's all."

"Ahead," she said. "Up a little. Be careful! Careful!"

And then, suddenly, it was there.

The instruments blazed with warning light, the air shrilling to the sound of the emergency alarm, overriding the cut-off in its desperate urgency. Acilus swore, strained at the controls, swore again as the *Mayna* creaked, opposed forces tearing at the structure.

Large in the screens loomed the bulk of a world, small, featureless, devoid of seas and mountains, bearing a scab of vegetation, an atmosphere, a city.

Chapter 11

It was cupped like a gem in the palm of surrounding hills, small and with a central spire which rose in a delicate cone. A spire which fell to mounds set in an intricate array each as smoothly finished as the shell of an egg. On them and the spire the light of the blue and yellow suns shone with rainbow shimmers so that Dumarest was reminded of a mass of soap bubbles, the light reflected as if from a film of oil.

"It's beautiful!" whispered Pacula. "Beautiful!"

She stood with the others on the summit of a low mound. The ship lay behind them in a clearing of its own making, a hacked path reaching from the mound to where it stood. To either side stretched a sea of vegetation; shoulder-high bushes bearing lacelike fronds, some in flower, others bearing fruit. Underfoot rested a thick carpet of mosslike undergrowth, broken stems oozing a pale-yellow sap.

The air was heavy, filled with a brooding stillness, the silence unbroken aside from their own sounds.

Embira said, "Earl! I'm afraid!"

"Be calm, dear." Pacula was soothing. "There's nothing to be afraid of."

An assurance born of ignorance. The vegetation could hold predators, the city enemies, the metallic taint in the air itself a warning of an abrupt, climatic change.

Sniffing at his pomander Jarv Nonach said dryly, "Well, we're here. What next?"

"We must investigate." Sufan Noyoka was impatient. "If anything of value is to be found it will be here. This city is the only artificial structure on the planet."

Or, at least, the only one they had been able to distinguish. An oddity in itself—normal cities did not stand in isolation—yet it was too large to be called a building, too elaborate to be called a village. Dumarest narrowed his eyes, studying the spire, the assembled mounds, his vision baffled by the shimmering light.

"It's deserted." Marek lowered his binoculars and handed them to Dumarest. "Empty."

Again an assumption which needn't be true. Dumarest adjusted the lenses and studied what he saw. The spire and mounds were featureless, unbroken by windows or decoration. The entire complex was ringed with a wall a hundred feet high, the ground around it bare for a width of two hundred yards. The soil was a dull gray, devoid of stones or vegetation, smooth aside from ripples which could have been caused by wind. The wall itself was unpierced by any sign of a door.

"Well?" Like Sufan Noyoka the captain was impatient. "Do we stand here and do nothing?"

"No."

"Then what?"

"We make an investigation." Dumarest lowered the binoculars. "Take the women back to the ship, Jarv also, and wait while we make a circuit of the city?"

"Why me?" The navigator was suspicious. "Why not Sufan?"

"The both of you."

"Earl?"

For answer Dumarest lifted his machete and cut at a mass of vegetation. Slashed leaves fell beneath the keen steel to reveal the slender bole. It parted to show a compact mass of fibers.

"Tough," he said flatly. "And neither of you is in good condition. We may have to run for it and you'll hamper us. Timus, Marek, and I will cut a path to the edge of the clearing and make a circuit of the city."

"We could follow you."

"Later, yes, but not now." As the man hesitated Dumarest added sharply, "We can't all go. The ship must be watched and the women protected." He added dryly, "Don't worry. If we find anything you'll know it."

The vegetation thickened a little as they descended the slope and it took an hour to cut a way to the clear area surrounding the wall. Dumarest halted at the rim of the clearing, kneeling to finger the soil, frowning as he looked at the clear line of demarcation. The dirt was gritty and felt faintly warm. The line was cut as if with a scythe, even the mossy undergrowth ending in a neat line.

"Earl?"

"Nothing." Dumarest rose, dusting his hands. As the engineer made to step out into the open he caught the man's arm. "No. We'll move around the edge and stay close to the vegetation."

"Why? The cleared ground will make the going easier."

"And reveal us to any who might be watching."

"There isn't anyone."

"We can't be sure of that."

"No," Timus admitted. "We can't. "But if there is they must have seen us land. Curiosity alone would have brought them outside or at least had them standing on the wall. Marek's right, Earl. The place is deserted."

And old. Dumarest could sense it as he led the way along the edge of the clearing. An impression heightened by the utter lack of sound, the intangible aura always associated with things of great antiquity. How long had it lain cupped in the palm of the hills? Given time enough it would vanish, buried beneath rain-borne dust, dirt carried by the winds, the broken leaves of the surrounding vegetation drifting to land, to rot and lift the surface of the terrain.

Thousand of years, millions perhaps, but it would happen.

Were other cities buried beneath the surface of this world?

Back at the ship Usan Labria said eagerly, "Well, Earl? What did you find?" She frowned as he told her. "Nothing? Just a city with no apparent way to get inside?"

"That's all." Dumarest drew water from a spigot and carried the cup back to the table around which they sat. The salon seemed cramped after the openness outside. "We made a complete circuit and studied the place from all directions. From each it looked the same."

"Balhadorha!" Timus snorted his disgust. "The world of fabulous treasure. The planet on which all questions are answered and all problems solved. So much for the truth of legend. All we have is an enigma."

"Which can be solved!" Sufan Noyoka was sharp. "What did you expect, men coming to greet us, giving us fortunes as a gift? A pit filled with precious metals or trees bearing priceless gems? Legend distorts the truth, but legend need not lie. Within that city could lie items of tremendous value."

If this world was Balhadorha. If the man hadn't followed a wrong lead and discovered a world not even hinted at in legend. A possibility Dumarest didn't mention as he sat, listening to the others.

"We've got to get inside and quickly!" Usan Labria was insistent. The last attack had almost killed her, the next might; she had no time to waste. Can you lift the ship and set it down beyond that wall?"

"On those mounds? No." The captain was blunt. "We need level ground."

"Climb it, then?" Pacula looked from one to the other "With ropes and pitons it should be possible."

"A hundred feet of sheer surface?" Timus shrugged. He was not a mountaineer.

"We could cut steps and make holds," she explained. "It shouldn't be hard. On Teralde, as a girl, I climbed higher slopes than that."

"I've a better suggestion," said Jarv Nonach from behind his pomander. "Let's blow a way in. With explosives we could break a hole in the wall."

"If it isn't too thick or too hard," agreed the engineer. Scowling he added, "We should have brought a raft with us. Well, it's too late to wish that now. Earl?"

"I suggest we wait. There is too much we don't know about this world as yet. To rush in might be stupid."

"Wait? For how long?" Usan bit at her lower lip. "And for what purpose? We aren't interested in anything aside from getting what we came to find. Blow the city to hell for all I care. Just let's get inside."

"And out again?" Dumarest set down his empty cup. "That's important, Usan, don't you think? To escape with the wealth we hope to find."

"Of course, but—" She broke off, making a helpless gesture. "You said the place was deserted."

"Marek said that, and I agree it seems that way, but we can't be sure. A delay won't do any harm."

A delay she couldn't afford, and others were equally impatient. A symptom of the danger Sufan had hinted at, the greed which blinded elementary caution.

"I say we blast a way in. Grab what we can and leave before anything can stop us." The navigator was definite. Sneeringly he added, "I'm not afraid of what I can't see if others are."

"I agree," said Acilus. "I didn't come here to start at shadows."

"We have to decide." Sufan Noyoka's eyes darted from one to the other. "Earl could be right to anticipate unknown dangers, but speed could be on our side. In any case we have no choice. How else to get within the city?"

Dumarest said quietly, "You're forgetting Marek Cognez."

"I'm glad someone remembered me." The man sat back in his chair, smiling. "To each his own. You, Captain, brought us here. You, Jarv, and you Sufan, guided us with some help from others. Earl warns us. I solve puzzles. And the city, as you said, Timus, is an enigma. One I find entrancing. Those who built it must have left. How? Did they have wings? The shape of the city is against it—level areas are needed for landing."

"Birds fly," said Pacula. "They don't need flat areas on which to land."

"True, but birds don't build cities. We couldn't spot anything which could have been a perch. And after landing, what then? Men do not walk on rounded surfaces and no creature finds it easy."

"There could be streets."

"True, we saw none but, I admit, they could be there. But think a moment. Imagine a city of mounds, not domes but structures shaped like eggs. Only the central spire shows straight lines. Logic tells us that the streets, if present, would be narrow and winding, overhung and unpleasant to walk on especially for a winged race. And the surrounding clearing, what of that? Earl studied it. Earl?"

"A radioactive compound with a long half-life would have sterilized the soil," he said.

"Yes, but why?" Marek looked from face to face. "A part of the puzzle and a question which should be answered. Given time I will answer it, but I must have time."

"We don't need answers," snapped the navigator. "Smash the wall and go in."

"And if the city isn't empty?"

"Kill those inside."

"If they can be killed. But think a moment. Does a man leave his house unguarded? If the city holds treasure it could be protected. If—"

"There are too many 'ifs.' " Rae Acilus slammed his hand

hard on the table. Marek, you say the city is deserted. Right?"

"As far as I can determine, yes."

"So we have nothing to worry about from what could be inside. Our only problem is the wall. We can climb it or blow a hole through it."

"Or burn one with lasers," said the engineer. "If it isn't too thick."

"A hundred feet high—it has to be thick. Now . . ."

Dumarest rose and left them arguing. Outside the blue sun was setting, the one of somber red lifting above the horizon. Here there could be no night or time of darkness—always one or more of the suns would ride in the sky.

Without the sight of stars would those who had lived here have ever guessed at the tremendous majesty of the universe? Had they grown introverted, using their skill and energy to turn one planet into a paradise instead of forming a thousand into living hells? Was that the basis of the legend, the moral truth it held?

But if people had lived here what had happened to them? Where were those who had built and lived in the city?

"Earl?" He turned. Embira had come to join him at the open port. "Is that you, Earl?"

"Yes, couldn't you tell?"

"The metal," she said. "Of the hull and that you wear. They merge—is it you?"

For answer he took her hands. They were cold, trembling, a quiver which grew as suddenly she pressed herself hard against him.

"Earl! Please!"

A woman lost and needing comfort. He held her close, one hand stroking the mane of her hair, the other about her shoulders. Suffused by her femininity it was hard to remember she was blind, that she couldn't see his face, his expression. That she knew him only as an aura distinguished by the metal he wore, the knife he carried.

"Earl!"

"I'm sorry." He eased the grip of his arm, a constriction born of protective tenderness. "Did I hurt you?"

"A little, but it was nice." She spoke with a warm softness. "Nice to feel you close to me, Earl. I feel safe when you are. Less afraid."

"Still afraid, Embira?"

"It's this place, this world. It is so empty and the sky so threatening. Will we be leaving soon?"

"Yes, soon."

"And then, Earl?" She waited for the answer she hoped to hear, one he could not give. "Will you stay with me? Will you?"

"For as long as necessary, Embira."

"I want you to stay with me for always. I never want to be without you. Earl, promise me that you will stay!"

"You should rest, Embira. You must be tired."

"And you?"

Deliberately he mistook her invitation. "I've work to do, Embira. I'm going to examine the area around the ship."

He walked a mile in a direct line from the city, cutting a path when the vegetation grew too dense, pausing often to listen, dropping at times to rest his ear against the ground. The stillness was complete.

A heavy, brooding silence which was unnatural. The vegetation provided good cover for game and there should have been small animals if not larger beasts, but he saw nothing, not even the trails such animals would have made. The air, too, was devoid of birds and he could spot no sign of insects. The bushes must be hybrids, propagating from roots alone, the flowers and fruits an unnecessary byproduct.

He cut one open and sniffed at the succulent mass of orange pulp. As he'd expected, it was seedless. The blooms were the size of his opened hand, waxen petals of a pale amber laced with black. Like the fruits they had no discernible odor.

The result of intensive cultivation, he decided, or a freak mutation which had spread to become dominant. The moss would be a saprophyte, feeding on decaying leaves fallen from the bushes. Dead animals would also provide food, and in the past perhaps, the moss had not waited for the beasts to die.

Back at the ship Dumarest learned a decision had been reached.

"Acilus is going to use explosives." Marek gestured toward the city. "He's taken Timus and Jarv with him and all are loaded with charges."

"The captain overrode my authority." Sufan Noyoka radiated his anger. "The man is a fool. Who knows what damage he might do? What treasures might be lost? Earl, if we could talk?"

He led Dumarest to one side, out of earshot of Marek and the two women who stood at the open port. Emibra, asleep, was in her cabin.

"I am worried about the captain, Earl," said Sufan quickly. "He holds the loyalty of the crew. If he should break into the city he might forget that I command this expedition."

"So?"

"Remember why you are here. The women will obey you—Marek too, perhaps—but if it comes to the need for action strike first and strike hard." The man bared his teeth, his face grown ugly. "I will not be cheated by greedy fools!"

"As yet you haven't been."

"No, but I am aware of the possibility. Go after them, Earl. If they breach the wall make them wait. I must be the first into the city."

As was his right, and Dumarest was content to let another be the target for any unexpected danger. As he strode down the hacked path Marek fell into step behind him.

"We tested the wall, Earl," he said. "While you were away. It is adamantine. Acilus hopes to penetrate it with shaped charges but I doubt if the ship carries enough to do the job." Pausing, he added, "They are armed."

With the weapons carried in the hold—the captain would have thought of that. Guns to kill anything in the city—or anyone who tried to stop him. Dumarest halted at the edge of the wide clearing. Against the wall Acilus was setting packages, Timus at his rear, the navigator to one side. Their voices carried through the still air.

"Set another just above the first. Not there, Jarv, you fool, there!"

"A heavy charge, Captain."

"We could need it. The detonators?"

"Here." Small in the distance Timus held them out, watched as Acilus thrust them home.

"The fuse," he rapped. "Quickly."

There was no obvious need for speed, but Dumarest guessed the loom of the blank wall must have unnerved him, the impression of watching eyes. He saw flame spring from the captain's hand, more flame sparkle from the length of black fuse.

"That's it. Now run!"

Dumarest joined them as they reached the trail, following as they ran to the mound, dropping behind its shelter. Marek dropped beside him. The engineer, panting for breath, said, "Fifty seconds. I've been counting. In less than a minute it will blow."

"Why didn't you use an electronic detonator?"

"We tried, Earl, it didn't work. Don't ask me why. I wanted to rig a launcher but the captain was impatient." Timus glanced to where Acilus crouched like an animal on the ground. "When he gets that way you can't argue with him. Thirty seconds."

A time unnecessarily short but one which dragged. Jarv Nonach wheezed, sniffed at his pomander, stared up at the sky.

"Five seconds." He frowned as they passed. "Minus three if I've counted right."

A navigator was accustomed to check the passage of time as a runner was of distance. His frown increased as still the charges didn't blow.

"Thirty seconds, Captain. You sure you set the detonators correctly?"

"Shut your mouth!" Acilus's tone revealed his doubt. "We'll give it a while longer."

Another three minutes during which his patience became exhausted.

"Give me another fuse and some more detonators," he snapped. "I'll fix this."

"No!" Dumarest rose to catch his arm. "Don't be a fool, man! Give it more time. What are you using, impact charges?"

"Safety plastic," said the engineer. "You could shoot a gun at it and it still wouldn't explode."

"Not if you hit a detonator?" Dumarest snatched the weapon from where it hung on the man's shoulder. "At least it's worth a try."

The gun was cheap, a rapid-fire light machine gun meant to be cradled in the arms, used to lay a rain of bullets without regard to accuracy. A short-range weapon good for street fighting but very little else. Dumarest lay on the summit of the mound, checked the sights, and fired a burst at the charges. He might as well have fired into empty air.

"You're wasting time," said Acilus. "'You could shoot all

day and never hit a thing. The fuse must have burned out. We'll have to fix another."

Dumarest fired again with no better result. As the magazine emptied he said, "Give me another."

"No!" The captin knocked aside the gun Jarv held upward. "We'll do it my way."

"Why bother?" Marek was bland. "There's a lot of wall," he reminded. "Why not move along it and try somewhere else?"

"No need. The charges are set. If the fuse hadn't burned out—"

"You can't be sure it did."

"To hell with you. I'm sure. Timus, Jarv, let's get at it!" Acilus sucked in his breath as neither moved. "Get on your feet, damn you! That's an order!"

Timus said, "We're not in space now, Captain. You want to risk your neck, that's your business."

"Jarv?" His eyes were murderous as the navigator shook his head. "So that's it. Cowards, the pair of you. I'll remember that."

Dumarest said, "Be sensible. Do as Marek suggests."

The final straw which broke the captain's hesitancy. "You!" he said. "By God, you overrode me once, you won't do it again. In space or on land I give the orders. Refuse to obey and it's mutiny. Remember that when we're back in space!"

A crime for which eviction was the penalty, a revenge Acilus would take later if he could. Dumarest watched as the man ran down the trail toward the edge of the clearing. Dust rose beneath his feet as he headed for the wall and the massed charges set and waiting. He reached them, busied himself with the fuse, and then, without warning, they blew.

A gush of flame blasted from the wall, dimming the suns, shaking the air with the roaring thunder of released destruction. Dumarest dropped, blinking to clear his eyes from retinal images, but there was no shower of debris.

When he looked again he could see nothing but a drifting plume of dust, a hole gouged in the ground, a wreath of smoke.

Acilus had vanished, blasted to atoms, and the wall reared as before, untouched, pristine.

Chapter 12

Timus Omilcar poured himself wine and said bitterly, "Over a hundred pounds of explosive and nothing to show for it but a hole in the ground and a missing captain. Want a drink, Earl?"

"That damned wall." The engineer lifted his glass, swallowed, sat scowling at the bottle. "We can't drive a pick into it, we can't touch it with lasers, and we can't blow a hole through it. The city's there—but how the hell do we get inside?"

A problem Dumarest was working on. From metal rods he had fashioned a grapnel, the tines curved, sharpened, a hook-eye supplied for a rope. He fitted it as Timus reached for the bottle.

"A hundred feet, Earl," he reminded. "A hell of a throw."

And no surety the tines would catch, but it had to be tried. At the foot of the wall Dumarest studied it, eyes narrowed against the glare of the red and yellow suns. With legs braced he swung the grapnel, threw it, the barbs hitting well below the summit of the smooth expanse. Another try threw it higher, a third and it was close to the top. On the second following try the hooked metal fell over the edge, to fall as Dumarest gently tugged at the rope.

A dozen attempts later he gave up. The summit of the wall was too smooth to offer a hold and he was sweating with the effort of casting the grapnel. Dropping the rope he rested the side of his face against the wall and studied the unbroken expanse. Light shimmered from it as if it had been polished. Even at the place blasted by the explosives it resembled the sheen of a mirror. Against his cheek it felt neither hot nor cold, the temperature equal to his own.

Entering the ship he heard voices raised in argument.

"Do you think I gimmick the fuse?" The engineer's voice was a roar. "Is that what you're saying?"

"I'm trying to understand." Usan Labria was sharp. "You gave him the detonators and fuses, right?"

"Yes."

"And you didn't go back with him when they failed to work. So—"

"So you think I refused because I knew the charges would blow? Woman, you're crazy! You know anything about explosives?"

"A little."

"Then listen. The stuff was safety plastic and you could hit it with a hammer and it would remain inert. Earl shot at it with no effect. The detonators were chemical-cascade; three units—the first blowing the second, the second the third, the third doing the job. "Got that?"

"The fuse?"

"Again chemical. Regular burn and normally you could set a watch by it, but things can happen. A fuse can volley—burn faster than expected, the flame jumping at accelerated speed. Or it can die, but when it does there's always the chance that it's still alive. The flame just moves slower, that's all. Acilus knew that but he was too damned impatient." Timus ended bleakly, "It cost him his life."

They were all in the salon aside from Embira, Usan Labria breathing deeply, the locket containing her drugs clutched in one hand. Pacula rose as Dumarest entered.

"I'd better go and look after the girl."

"Leave her." Marek toyed with his cards. "She isn't a baby."

"She's blind. Have you forgotten?"

"We're all blind when asleep, my dear." He turned three cards, pursed his lips, then gathered up the deck. "You worry about her too much."

"And you too little."

"Not so." Marek smiled, his teeth, sharp and regular, flashing in the light. "I think of her often and, when she is close, it is easy to forget her disability. Her charms negate her lack of vision and it would be no handicap. After all, are not fingers the eyes of the night?"

"You're vile!"

"No, my dear," he said blandly. "Not vile—human. She is a woman, is she not? And I am a man."

"Degenerate filth!" She stood looking down at him, her

eyes cold. "I warn you, Marek Cognez. If you touch her
I'll—"

"Do what?" He rose to face her, his eyes as hard and bleak
as her own. "You threaten me? That is a challenge I am
tempted to accept. And if I should take the girl what could
you do? Nothing. Nothing."

"Perhaps not," said Dumarest. "But I could. Touch Embira and you'll answer to me."

"A challenge multiplied." For a moment Marek held his
eyes, and then abruptly, shrugged and smiled. "You make the
odds too great, Earl. A woman, what is that to come between
friends? And we are friends, are we not?"

Dumarest said, "Pacula, if you're going to the girl go
now." As she left the salon he sat and looked at Marek. "One
day you'll go too far. And you're wrong about Pacula not
being able to take revenge. Any woman can use a knife
against a man when he is asleep. She may not kill you, but
she could ruin your face and teach you what it is to be
blind."

"And you, Earl?"

"I'd kill you."

A cold statement of fact which the man accepted for what
it was. Even so, the devil within him forced him on.

"An interesting development, Earl. Had another man made
that threat I would assume him to be in love with the girl. Or
are you anticipating the future and the enjoyment of unsul-
lied goods?"

Timus said quickly, "Be careful, Marek."

"Another warning? This seems to be a time of warnings.
Even the cards are full of dire prophecy. A pity the captain
had no trust in my skill. But then—one less and the more to
share."

"The more of what?" Jarv Nonach gestured with his pomander. "As yet we have found nothing, and unless we can
break through the walls, we'll remain empty-handed. Did you
have any luck?"

"No," admitted Dumarest.

"Then what is left?" The navigator looked from one to the
other. "I say we should leave here and return later with rafts
and—"

"No!" Sufan's hand slammed on the table. "No!"

"What point in staying? With the captain dead I am in
command of the *Mayna*. I am a fair man and as eager as any

of you to find treasure, but the wall beats us. How long are we to sit looking at it? I say we leave. With rafts and other equipment we could crack that city open like a nut."

"We stay!" Sufan Noyoka was trembling with passion. "To have come so far, to have risked so much—we stay!"

"For a little longer." The navigator rose, his face drawn, determined. "But not for too long. I command the *Mayna* now and when I leave you may come or stay as you wish."

Dumarest said, "We are partners, Jarv. Sufan Noyoka leads this expedition."

"Then why doesn't he accept the obvious? It's our lives as well as his. Acilus is dead—how many more must follow him? Without equipment we haven't a chance. No, Earl, I've decided. One more day and then I leave."

A threat he might have carried out had he been allowed, but when the blue sun rose and the yellow sank he was dead.

Dumarest heard the cry and was running, catching Usan Labria as she fell, following the finger of her pointing hand.

"Earl," she gasped. "I found him. The navigator—under that bush."

She was quivering, her lips blue, pain contorting her raddled features. Dumarest passed her to Timus as he came running, Marek at his side.

"Earl?"

"Take her back to the ship. Get hold of Pacula, she knows what to do."

"And Jarv?"

"I'll see what's wrong."

There was nothing he could do. The man sat with his back against a bole, his head slumped forward down on his chest, one hand clenched at his side, the other open, the pomander lying an inch from his fingers. Dumarest halted Marek as he moved forward.

"Wait. Look around. See if you can spot tracks of any kind."

"On this moss?"

"The stems could be broken. Look."

A heavy weight would have left an impression but nothing could be found aside from the marks of the navigator's footprints and those left by Usan and themselves. Dumarest quested in a wide circle, frowning as he rejoined Marek.

"Nothing?"

"No."

"Which means nothing jumped him from the vegetation," mused Marek. "He must have come out here to sit, maybe to think and plan, resting his back against the bole and then something happened. But what? There seems to be no sign of a struggle. Poison of some kind? Those blooms, Earl! The bush he is under bears blossom. Could they have emitted a lethal vapor of some kind?"

"Perhaps." Dumarest glanced at the sky. This world was strange, beneath the varying influence of the suns anything could happen. "Be careful now, don't get too close."

Holding his breath he lifted the dead man's face. It was tranquil, the open eyes glazed, the lips slightly parted. The skin was cool and a little moist. Death had come quickly.

Marek said, "Shall we bury him, Earl?"

"If you want to, go ahead."

"And you?"

"I've work to do in the ship."

A plan he had made and devices he and the engineer had worked on while the others rested. The navigator was dead—left or buried, to him it was the same, but the living still faced a problem.

"Do you think they'll work, Earl?" Timus looked dubiously at what they'd made; soft hemispheres of rubber backed by a stronger layer and fitted with loops. Gekko pads to fit to wrists, elbows, knees, and ankles, any six of the suction cups sufficient to hold his weight.

"It's a chance," said Dumarest. "The wall is smooth and the cups should hold if we figured right."

"If they don't we're stuck, Earl. I don't know what else we can do. Jarv was right in a way. We need rafts and special equipment. Sufan Noyoka should have thought about it. Well, it's too late now, but maybe Jarv had the right idea. You burying him?"

"Marek's seeing to it." Dumarest anticipated the obvious question. "No sign of what killed him, but he went peacefully."

"His heart must have given out." Timus rubbed his hand over his chin. "He was always sniffing at that pomander and it was only a matter of time before the drugs got him. "Two down," he said. "And it's my guess the old woman will be next."

Pacula was with her, sitting beside the cot, bathing the

raddled face with water. Usan's breathing was labored, her fingers twitching, plucking at her dress. Weakly she tried to smile.

"Age, Earl. It's beating me. Jarv?"

"Dead and being buried. His heart must have given out. There was no sign of any attack." Dumarest touched the woman's throat, his fingers resting on the pulse. "We don't want you going the same way. It would be best for you to sleep for a while. Pacula?"

"I'll see to it, Earl."

"No!" Usan clenched her hands, eyes brimming with tears at her own weakness. "Damn this body! I don't want to sleep. I want to see what's in the city."

"If we manage to get inside you'll be with us. That's a promise."

"You're kind," she whispered. "I'll hold you to that. But can you get inside?"

Dryly he said, "There's only one way to find out."

Sufan Noyoka's dry voice issued a list of instructions as they headed toward the wall.

"Remember to fix the rope as soon as you reach the top, Earl. Make no attempt to get into the city until I am with you. Are you armed?"

"He's armed." Timus handed Dumarest a machine gun. "Hang this around your neck, Earl. It's cocked and ready to fire on full automatic."

Dumarest weighed it in his hand then handed it back.

"I'll pull it up if and when I reach the top," he said. "I've enough weight to carry as it is."

His own body, the pads, the rope wrapped around his waist, the grapnel swinging between his shoulders. Reaching the foot of the wall he looked upward. Every spot was the same and one was as good as another. As the others watched he stepped close to the smooth expanse, lifted his arms, slammed the pads against the wall, followed with a leg. With the pads holding he lifted his free leg and set it higher than the other. Then an arm pulled free, lifted and made fast. The other leg. The other arm. A leg again.

Slowly, sprawled hard against the wall, each limb moving in turn, he inched upward.

He could see nothing but the wall inches from his eyes, feel nothing but the drag at his arms, the awkward twist of his legs. Each time he freed a pad meant a cautious twisting, to fasten them a careful movement. Sweat began to run from his forehead into his eyes and he felt the clammy touch of it beneath his clothing.

Grimly he climbed on, inches at a time, muscles aching in thighs and groin, cramps threatening his shoulders and calves.

From below came the encouraging voice of the engineer.

"Keep going, Earl! You're doing fine!"

"How high am I?"

"Maybe thirty feet!"

Less than a third of the distance covered. Thirty feet out of a hundred and already the strain of hauling his body up the sheer wall was beginning to tell. Pausing, Dumarest hung to rest, turning his head to see the sea of vegetation, the ship rearing against the sky. The light from the suns was dazzling, reflected from the wall it hurt his eyes. Closing them he released one leg, flexing it to ease the strain.

"Up!" snapped Sufan Noyoka. "Earl, what are you waiting for?"

Dumarest made no answer, easing each limb in turn, then doggedly continued to climb. At sixty feet progress slowed, the pads seeming to slip, and after another five feet he was sure of it. Watching, he placed his arm into position, heaved, saw the attachments move down the wall as if they glided on oil.

Cautiously he moved to one side, tried to climb again but with no better result. Tilting his head he looked at the top of the wall. He was two-thirds of the way up, a little more and he would be home, but the last few feet were impossible to cover.

Timus caught him as he dropped from the wall.

"Earl? Are you all right?"

"Cramp." Dumarest doubled, kneading his legs. His shoulders ached and his arms burned. He had climbed mountains with less bodily fatigue. "Maybe something in the wall. I don't know."

"So you failed." Sufan was bitter. "A few more feet, couldn't you make it?"

"I tried." For too long and too hard. The red sun was setting, the yellow taking its place. "The wall won't hold the suction cups up there. They slip."

"And?"

Dumarest shrugged. "I don't know. Maybe Marek has an idea."

"He sat as usual in the salon, toying with his cards, his face smooth, apparently unconcerned, but one whose brain was never still. A man who had boasted of his talent, one who had now to prove his claims.

"A problem," he said. "A puzzle, and each tackles it in his own way. Acilus tried brute force, you were more subtle, Earl, but with no greater success. Yet such attempts had to be made and the use of suction cups was clever. A lighter person, perhaps? But no. You alone have to have the physical attributes necessary for such a climb. What else? Well, first let us study the situation."

"We've done that," said Sufan curtly. "A city locked behind a wall."

"Exactly, a wall." Marek turned some cards, his eyes bland. "Now, what is a wall? It is a barrier set to keep others out. But that same barrier will keep others in. Perhaps the city is a prison built to contain some criminal form of life. A possibility, you must admit, and one which must be considered. For while every prison must have a key it is equally true to state that no prison can be entered without it having a door."

"I have no patience to listen to abtruse meanderings, Marek."

"Yet patience in this matter is essential. Earl advised it, Acilus rejected it, and by so doing, lost his life. Jarv also was impatient and Jarv is dead." His voice hardened a little to take on an edge. "I have no wish to join them, Sufan. Not yet. And not because you refuse to wait."

"Then tell us how to enter the city."

"Find the door."

"What?" Sufan frowned, his eyes coming to rest, sharp in their anger. "I warn you, Marek—"

"Again a warning!" Marek threw down the cards. "I grow tired of warnings. You have seen what I have seen, know what I know. The city is an enigma. To understand it I must study it. Why are the mounds set in such a fashion? What is the purpose of the spire? Why is the wall so high and why does its surface alter toward the summit? Why the clearing?"

"That is to keep the vegetation from growing too close to the wall. That's obvious."

"But not necessarily true." Marek leaned back, resting the tips of his fingers together, an attitude Dumarest found at varience to his character.

He said, without irony, "Is the puzzle too simple, Marek?"

"Earl, you have it! What could be more simple than an apparently impenetrable wall? You, at least, do not fall into the common error of believing that complexity makes for difficulty. The reverse is true; the more complex a thing, the more parts there are in relation to each other, the more simple it is to determine an answer. Find me the door and I will lead you into the city. But first I must locate the door."

"But how?" Timus was baffled. "We've looked, there is no door. Earl?"

Dumarest said, "You think about it, Timus. I need a shower."

Embira was waiting as he stepped from the cubicle. She wore a close-fitting gown of silver laced with gold, a perfect accompaniment to her skin and hair. She moved toward him, one hand trailing the wall.

"Earl?"

"Yes." He took her hand. "I thought you were asleep."

"I was, but I've rested long enough. Take me outside, Earl. The metal," she gestured toward the hull, "cramps me."

Outside the air was brooding with a heavy stillness, the sky painted with a profusion of light. The red sun was low on the horizon, the yellow on its upward climb, the blue barely visible. Three suns that bathed the city with light. From the summit of the mound Dumarest looked at it, then at the girl. She was frowning.

"Something wrong?"

"What is out there, Earl? What do I face?"

"The city. You have seen—faced it before." Curious, he added, "Can you krang the wall?"

"The wall? No. There is only something—" She broke off, shivering. "Something I don't understand. It isn't familiar, Earl. I don't like it."

"The wall, Embira." He took her head between his hands and guided her sightless eyes along its length. "Can you isolate it as you can the hull?" He frowned at her answer. "No?"

"No, Earl. But there is something there." She pointed with her arm. "I can krang it. It isn't like what lies beyond." She added uncertainly, "I can't remember it being there before."

A manifestation of the triple suns? If so, time was limited, there was no way of knowing when all three would be in the sky at the same time again. A mistake? If so, nothing could be lost by trying.

Back at the ship Marek said incredulously, "A door? Earl, are you sure?"

"No, but it's worth the chance. Embira spotted something, an alteration. We must investigate. Get the others and follow."

"But—"

"Hurry! The red sun's setting. Once it has gone the chance could be lost!"

A chance which seemed less possible the closer they approached the wall. It hadn't changed. At close hand it seemed as firm and as unbroken as before. To normal eyes, at least, but Embira lacked normal vision. Walking steadily in the lead she made directly toward a certain point. Dumarest, Usan Labria cradled in his left arm, followed. From the rear of the little column the engineer voiced his doubts.

"A door? Earl, that wall's solid. How the hell can we pass through it?"

"Walk. It's a chance, but what have we to lose? Embira will guide us. Touch the one in front, close your eyes, and follow." Dumarest set the example, resting his free hand on the girl's shoulder. Behind him Pacula sucked in her breath and he felt the touch of her hand.

"Like this, Earl?"

"Yes. All in contact? Then close your eyes."

The dirt underfoot was smooth, there was no danger of stumbling, and Dumarest made a conscious effort to forget the presence of the wall. It didn't exist. Nothing existed aside from the warmth of the flesh beneath his hand, the body of the girl in the lead. The blind leading the blind—but she had her talent, and without vision, they were more crippled than she.

Five steps, ten, twelve. Dumarest concentrated on the girl. Another three steps, five, seven—and he felt a mild tingle. Eight more and the girl halted.

"Earl. It's behind us. The thing I could krang."

A risk, but it had to be taken. Dumarest opened his eyes.

Behind him he heard Pacula gasp, Marek's voice, high, incredulous.

"By God, we've done it! We've passed through the door! We're in the city!"

Chapter 13

They stood in a vast chamber, the curved roof high above suffused with an opalescent sheen of light; colored gleams which filled the place with broken rainbows. The floor was smooth, polished, made of some adamantine material, seamless and traced with a pattern of sinuous lines. The curved wall was pierced with a rounded opening several times the height of a man.

"The entrance hall." Marek's voice was clear, the place devoid of echoes as it was of shadows. "The area beyond the door, and we're in it."

But not all. Dumarest said, "Where's Timus?"

"He was behind me." Sufan Noyoka looked up, around, down toward the floor. "I felt his hand slip from my shoulder. I don't know just when."

Before he had reached the wall, his own eyes and disbelief maintaining the barrier. In Dumarest's arms Usan Labria stirred, muttering, still fogged with sleep-inducing drugs. Her eyes cleared as he held a vial beneath her nostrils, crushing the ampul and releasing chemical vapors to clear her blood.

"Earl?"

"It's all right," he soothed. "We're in the city."

"The city!" She freed herself from his support and stood, looking around. "Yes," she whispered. "We must be. You kept your promise, Earl. My thanks for that. But how?"

"Embira guided us."

"Blind, she couldn't see the wall," explained Marek. "But she sensed the presence of a force field of some kind. A means to open the matter of the wall, perhaps, while maintaining the illusion it was solid. A door built on a unique pattern. One which—" He broke off, shrugging. "Does it matter? We're inside, that's all that counts."

"Inside!" She drew a deep breath and squared her shoulders, summoning the dregs of her energy. Impatiently she

111

brushed aside Pacula's hand. "Don't coddle me, girl. I'll be all right. Stay with Embira, she'll need a guide." She frowned, aware of the absence of the engineer. "Timus?"

"He isn't with us," said Sufan. "He must still be outside, but it is of no importance. Alone he can't handle the *Mayna*. All he can do is wait."

Wait as the colored suns traced their path across the sky, alone in the brooding silence, faced with the blank enigma of the city. How long would he remain patient? Dumarest lacked Sufan's conviction that the engineer was helpless. A clever man could rig remote controls and, desperate, Timus might try to navigate the Cloud on his own. A gamble which he couldn't win, but one he would try given time enough.

Stepping to the wall, Dumarest rested his hand on the surface. It felt as before, neither hot nor cold, the material solid against his pressure.

"Embira, has anything changed?"

"The aura has gone, Earl." She faced him as he stood against the wall. "I can krang another, more distant."

The bulk of the vessel containing the residual energies of the field. While she could discern it they had a point of directional reference—but until the door opened again they were trapped unless they could find another way to leave the city.

Sufan shrugged when Dumarest mentioned it.

"We'll find a way, Earl. Now let us see what is to be found."

"But with caution," warned Marek. "The door could have given an alarm and the city might still contain some form of life. It would be as well to move carefully."

A conclusion Dumarest had already reached. All, aside from Embira and the old woman, carried packs, canteens, and were armed. He checked the gun hanging on its strap from his shoulder.

"If we see anything hold your fire. If we are attacked wait until I shoot. Marek, you take the rear, Sufan, you stay with the women."

"I will—"

"Do as he says, Sufan," snapped Usan. "One of us at least must keep a clear head. We've come too far to be beaten now and an error could cost us all our lives." She sucked in her breath and fumbled at her locket, slipping a pill between her lips. "But hurry, Earl. Hurry!"

They moved toward the opening, feeling like ants in a

cathedral, stunned by the vastness of the chamber. Another
opened beyond, smaller, set with an opening through which
smooth ramps led up and down. Their roofs were of some
lustrous substance which threw a nacreous glow. The air was
thick, slightly acrid. Dumarest could see no trace of dust.

"An entrance hall," mused Marek. "Ramps which must
lead to other chambers. Assuming this place held life similar
to ours there will be living accommodation and recreational
areas."

"Up or down?"

"Up, Earl. Below must lie machines and storerooms, cess
pits, perhaps, a means of sewage disposal. Already the pattern begins to take form. Give me time and I will draw a
map of the city."

"We want the treasure," said Usan Labria. "Just the
treasure."

"Then we must head toward the central spire." Marek
stepped toward one of the openings. "This one, Earl."

A guess, but it was as good as any, and Dumarest led the
way toward it. The ramp rose steeply after a hundred feet
then leveled as it broke into another chamber also set with
openings. A series of them so that, within minutes, they
passed through a maze of connecting rooms all appearing exactly alike.

Pacula said uncertainly, "We could become lost. How can
we be sure of finding the way back?"

"We're not lost." Marek was confident. "Always we take
the central opening and climb upward."

"This reminds me of something." Usan looked around,
frowning. "A bee hive? No. An ant hill? An ant hill! Earl!
This place is like an ant hill."

Short passages and endless chambers all alike, none with
distinctive characteristics. A prison was like that, a place built
for a strictly utilitarian function without concession to art-
istry. The mere fact of living in such a place would mold the
residents into a faceless whole, all individuality repressed by
the endless monotony of the surroundings. Men, held in such
an environment, would become abnormal.

Had the city been built by men?

There was no way of telling. A single chair would have
given a clue as to shape and form, a table, a scrap of decoration, but the chambers were devoid of all furnishings, the

openings providing the only break in the seamless construction, the sole decoration that of the sinuous lines.

They ran thin and black against the pale gray of the floor, following no apparent order, twisting to bunch into knots, opening to splayed fans.

Directional signs? A means to tell the inhabitants exactly where they were in the city?

"It's possible, Earl," admitted Marek when Dumarest spoke of it. "We have street signs and numbers, insects have scent-trails; whoever built this place could have had their own system. But to break the cipher would take too long. And it isn't necessary. All we have to do is to reach the spire."

And the treasure if treasure was to be found. But five hours later they were still no closer to where it might be.

"We're lost!" Sufan Noyoka glared his impatience. "So much for your skill, Marek. Give me time, you said, and you would produce a map of the city. Well?"

"A delay." Marek spread his hands, smiling, but his tone was sharp. "Do you expect a miracle? Those who built this place were clever. The chambers, the passages, all follow a mathematical precision designed to confuse. There are subtle turns and windings."

Dumarest said, "How far are we from the gate?"

"Who can tell? Without any point of orientation—"

"You don't know." Dumarest turned to Embira. "Can you krang the ship?"

"It lies in that direction." Her lifted hand pointed to an opening to the right of the one they had used.

"And the other?" Dumarest caught her shoulders and gently turned her to face in the opposite direction. "Can you see—krang anything?"

"Yess." She shivered, suddenly afraid. "Earl, I don't like it. It's strange, and somehow, menacing. Like some of the auras in the Cloud."

"A force field, Embira? An entity?"

"I'm not sure. Earl! Hold me!"

"Stop tormenting her!" said Pacula. "You know she is upset. We should have left her behind in the ship."

"We had no choice," said Dumarest. "Without her we would never have passed through the wall. And, without her to help us, we may never be able to leave the city."

"Earl?"

"Think about it," he snapped. "We are lost. The chambers form a maze and Marek admits he can't find his way back despite what he said at first. Only Embira can guide us."

"To the ship?"

"That and more." Gently he said to the girl, "Now try, Embira. Tell us in which way to go. Point with your hand and aim at the aura you see ahead."

"Earl! It hurts! I—"

"Try, girl! Try!"

Stare into the glow of a searchlight, the glare of a sun— how could he tell what it was like? But he had to use familiar analogies in order to even begin to understand her attribute.

"Earl!" Don't! You can't hurt her like this!"

"Shut up, Pacula!" snapped Usan, and caught at her arm as she lunged forward. "Don't interfere! Let Earl handle things."

He said soothingly, "Just point, Embira. Just show us the way. Can you stop looking—kranging, if you want?"

To drop a mental shutter as a man would close an eye against too bright a light. An ability she must have if not to be driven insane by the pressure of surrounding auras.

"Yes, Earl. I have to concentrate. I—sometimes—there!" Her hand lifted, aimed at a point ahead and down. "There!"

"Is it close?"

"Closer than it was, Earl."

So Marek had not been a total failure. Dumarest stepped to the opening closet to where the girl had pointed. Beyond lay another chamber, more openings, one with a ramp leading downward. Again a featureless room, more openings, another extension of the maze.

He pressed on until he felt confused.

"Embira?"

"There." More calmly now she lifted her hand. "That way, Earl."

They had diverged from the path. Dumarest found it again, striking out and down, finally coming to a halt before a blank wall. Openings ran to either side, one ramp leading up, the other down. A hundred feet down the slope Embira paused.

"We're going the wrong way, Earl. The aura lies behind us."

"The passage could turn." Sufan Noyoka was impatient.

"There could be another junction lower down. Hurry, let us find it."

"We're running like rats in a sewer," said Usan irritably. "Slow down, Sufan. Earl?"

"We'll go back."

"And waste more time?" Sufan bared his teeth. "The girl can guide us once we reach another chamber."

"She is guiding us. We'll go back."

Facing the blank wall, Dumarest said, "Point again, Embira. Marek, mark the direction of her hand. Good. I'm going to try something." He lifted the gun to his shoulder, aimed at where the girl had pointed. "Maybe these walls can be penetrated. The rest of you had better leave the chamber in case of ricochets. Pacula, warn the girl what I am about to do."

Marek said, "Two guns could be better than one, Earl."

Twice the fire-power, but twice the risk from wildly ricocheting bullets.

Dumarest said, "I'm protected, you're not. Go with the others."

As he left Dumarest opened fire.

The gun kicked against his shoulder as a stream of heavy slugs blasted from the muzzle to slam against the wall. Some ricocheted to whine like angry wasps through the chamber, one catching his back to rip his tunic, bruising the flesh, only the metal mesh buried in the plastic saving him from an ugly wound. Beneath the storm of metal the wall crumbled to show a small, jagged opening. Again Dumarest fired, swinging the barrel in a rough circle. A kick and shattered fragments rained to lie in a heap on the floor.

"Did it work?" Marek came running as the gun fell silent. He glanced at the opening. "Earl, you did it! I thought—"

"The wall would be as adamantine as the one surrounding the city?"

"Yes. A natural assumption. How did you know it would yield?"

"I didn't, but it was worth the chance." Dumarest fitted a fresh magazine to the gun. "Let's see what lies beyond."

They stared at a long, oval chamber, the roof softly glowing, the walls pierced with circular openings bright with red and yellow sunlight. The floor was thick with a heavy layer of dust, and on it lay the body of a man.

He rested as if asleep, one arm extended, the fingers

curved. Only one cheek was visible, the face sunken, wreathed with a short beard. The eyes were open, glazed, the lips parted to show blunt and yellowed teeth. He wore a uniform of dull plastic, touches of green bright against the dark maroon, the colors barely visible through a coating of dust.

"A man," said Usan Labria. "And dead—but for how long?"

"Long enough." Marek stooped and brushed away the dust. More had drifted to form a low ridge around the body. "Centuries, perhaps. He's mummified."

"How did he die?" Pacula stepped close to the girl and threw an arm protectively around her shoulders. "Are there signs of wounding?"

"Does he carry papers?" Sufan Noyoka frowned as he stared at the corpse. "Look, man," he snapped as Marek hesitated. "He's dead. He can't hurt you."

"Maybe not." Marek was acid. "But what killed him could. Disease, perhaps?"

"Not disease," said Dumarest. "My guess is he died of starvation or thirst." Turning the body over he searched the pockets. "Captain Cleeve Inchelan," he read. "His ship the *Elgret*. The date—" He looked up at the ring of attentive faces. "Three hundred years ago."

"And his crew?" Usan looked from one to the other. "What happened to his crew? His ship? We saw no ship."

"Lost in the Cloud, maybe," said Marek. "Or maybe they managed to get back and spread rumors. The treasure planet," he added bitterly. "The Ghost World. Well, there is one ghost at least, if such things exist. That of Captain Inchelan."

A man who could also have followed a dream, searching for a fabled world and the treasure it was reputed to hold. Or had he given birth to the legend? His crew making a safe landing there to spread rumor and wild imaginings?

Dumarest said, "How did he get into the city? How did he get here?"

"A raft?" Marek was quick to catch the implication. "Of course, Earl! How else? But why here?" His eyes searched the dust, lifted to one of the circular openings. "They must give to the open air," he said. "How else the dust? Maybe the raft is outside. If it is we could use it."

"After three centuries?" Usan Labria shook her head. "No."

"Why not? From the look of the dust there is little climatic variation here. The raft could be unharmed. If we could find it—Earl!"

Together they reached the circular window. Dumarest jumped, caught the lower edge, hung while Marek swarmed up his body, heaved himself upward in turn. Beyond lay a level area, the surface of the dust unbroken.

"The other side, perhaps?" Marek dropped and crossed the oval chamber. Again they looked through an opening. "Nothing. He didn't leave it here, Earl."

Dumarest said, "He needn't have come alone. There could have been others."

"Who left him to starve?"

"Why not—if they had found treasure."

"Earl, you are a man with little trust in human nature, or perhaps one with too much knowledge of the power of greed. Is that what you think happened?"

"There is another possibility," said Dumarest. "He could have got lost. The raft could be somewhere in the city. He could have been looking for it and died before he found it." He added grimly, "As we could die. Our food and water is limited."

"You're worried about us being able to leave the city," said Marek. "You're concerned about the women. You surprise me, Earl. I would not have thought you afflicted with such hampering considerations. What will happen if we can't escape? Will you give them our rations? If that is your intention you could be due for a struggle. Sufan will let nothing stand in his way. Their lives mean nothing to him against the treasure."

"And you?"

"Earl, I will be honest. I came to find the treasure."

"And we may find it," said Dumarest. "But first we rest and eat."

The blue sun had risen when again they moved, a violet light blending with that of dull ruby, streamers of brilliance shrouding the dead man and reflecting from his staring eyes. His hand, extended after them, seemed to hold a silent plea, an appeal for help they could not give. The aid they carried had come centuries too late, the food and water which could have saved his life.

"That poor man," said Pacula somberly as they walked

toward the end of the oval chamber. "Dying like that, alone on an alien world."

"Left by his crew." Usan paused, coughing, flecks of red staining her lips. "Damn this dust. Earl, will it be long now?"

"Not long. We must be close to the central spire."

"And after? When we've found the treasure?" She coughed again, then said, "I'm not a fool. We're in the city but how do we get out? The girl can guide us back to the wall but how do we get through it?"

"We'll get through it," said Dumarest. "The same way we came in."

"By waiting at the right place for the right time. And when will that be? A week? A month? I—"

"You worry too much," he said curtly. "Just think about staying on your feet. Can you manage?"

"I'll manage," she said. "I'm going to find that treasure even if I have to crawl. What will it be, Earl? Gems? Ingots of precious metals? Some new device? A fortune anyway. We'll all make a fortune and I'll—take care of the girl, Earl. Without Embira we're lost. Take damned good care of her."

"I will."

"Yes," she said, and then flatly, "are you in love with her?" Her smile was a grimace as he made no answer. "She's in love with you, Earl. The poor, blind bitch, I feel sorry for her and yet—" She broke off, looking at her hands. "And yet," she whispered, "I'd give my soul to have her body."

Chapter 14

The chamber ended in a combination of smoothly concave surfaces blending into the mouth of a rounded opening giving on to more chambers, different this time, larger, the thin tracery of black lines almost covering the floor in their elaborate profusion. A ramp led up from the dust and again they plunged into a maze, simple this time, the walls forming broken barriers between chambers which grew higher and wider as they progressed.

Embira paused, wincing, one hand lifting to her forehead.

"Close," she whispered. "Earl, it's so close!"

"In which direction?" He followed the gesture of her hand. "Blank it out, Embira, if you can. Stop hurting yourself."

"Earl, you care?"

"Need you ask?" His hand closed on her own. "We need you, girl."

From behind them Sufan Noyoka said, "Hurry. The treasure must be close. Hurry!"

"Why?" Usan Labria leaned against a wall, panting for breath. "No one is going to steal it, Sufan. No one but us."

"If there's anything to steal. Our dead captain could already have emptied the nest." Marek was cynical. "Prepare yourself for a disappointment, my friend. We could be too late."

A reminder which the man didn't appreciate. He snapped, "Don't try to be funny, Marek. Use your talent. If it has any value you should be able to tell us the location of the treasure."

"Why ask me when we have the girl? Can't she tell us, Earl?"

"She's done enough," said Dumarest. "And she has never claimed to be able to solve puzzles. That is why you are here."

"That's right, Marek, or did you come just for the ride?"

Pacula, in defense of the girl, was quick to attack. "It's your turn to guide us."

"And I shall. Did you guess that I was proud? To be ignored can be hurtful to a man of talent. Given time I would have guided you, but I was not given time. And it amused me to know that, at any time, danger could have awaited in each and every chamber. A complication which, so far, we have been spared. But consider, my friends, would treasure be left unguarded?"

A question posed without need of an answer and Dumarest wondered at the spate of words. Was the man simply wasting time in order to gain an opportunity to arrange his thoughts? Or was he pressing their patience, risking anger and potential violence? A facet of his character which could never be forgotten. His whim could lead them into danger for the thrill of it. To toy with death to assuage his secret yearning.

Pacula said, "Must we have a lecture?"

"You want a simple answer?" His sudden anger was the flash of a naked blade. "There!" His hand lifted to point ahead. "At the heart of the city you will find the treasure—if it is to be found."

"You doubt?"

"Everything. Your smile, my dear, your greed, you concern. Nothing is wholly what it seems. This city, a place built for men or for what? Built to house or to hold? To guard or to retain? Every coin has two faces—must we only look at the one we find most pleasing to our eyes? Solve me a puzzle, you say, and do it now. Am I a dog to be ordered at your whim?"

An old wound opened by an unthinking comment. Dumarest said, "We need your skill, Marek."

"Have I denied it?"

"Then tell us, in your own way, what you have determined."

"Let us talk of treasure." Marek sat and took a sip of water from his canteen. From the way he tilted it Dumarest knew that the contents must be low. "What is treasure? To one it could be a bag of salt, to another a bow, a knife, a prime beast. Values vary, so what do we hope to find?"

"Money," said Usan curtly. "Or something we can turn into money."

"Works of art? A discovery which can be carried in the

the mind or a heap of stone a hundred men couldn't lift?"

"You try my patience!"

"The voice of aggression," he said calmly. "Who are you not to be denied? A woman, old, dying. What challenge do you offer? None. And you Sufan. You too are old and consumed by greed. Why should I obey you? How can you make me?"

Dumarest said, "He can't. No one can. Now tell us what you know."

For a moment Marek remained silent, then he said in an altered tone of voice, "For you, Earl, yes. At least you are a man, and I think, one with understanding. Now consider this. Where in a normal city would you find the greatest concentration of treasure? On a commerical world it would be figures in a ledger or items in a computer—the interflow of credit and debit. A more primitive world and metal and gems would be stored in some vault. A religious one and the altar of the largest place of worship would be garnished with things of price. A military world would value weapons. An artistic one volumes of poetry, perhaps, or paintings."

"So?"

"The consideration determines the keeping. Now some rumors have it that the wealth of Balhadorha is the loot of a ravished world. The wealth of a planet heaped like a mass of stone, dumped and left to be found by any with the courage to look for it. We know better. It must be at the heart of this city. But is it large or small? If small then it could be anywhere within the central spire. If large then at or below ground level. Was it to be seen? Adored or examined, touched by the populace, or something hidden?"

Dumarest said, "The chambers we passed through were all devoid of ornament."

"A shrewd observation. Which leads us to the conclusion that the inhabitants of this city had no time for artistic appreciation. Perhaps they were incapable of it. And they must have left centuries ago—otherwise they would not have permitted the dead man to remain where we found him. Where did they go and why did they leave?"

"If they left at all," said Dumarest. "But we're not interested in the city as such, only the treasure."

"But all are parts of the puzzle." Marek took another drink of water. "Down," he said. "I am sure of it. Down and at the center. It will be found, I am sure, at a point below the present ground level." Smiling, he added, "If there is anything there to find."

One day, thought Dumarest, the man's sense of humor would kill him. He would take one chance too many and the death he was in love with would reach out and take him. As Marek led the way Dumarest glanced at the others. Pacula, as had grown normal, guided the girl. Usan panted, coughing, her eyes bloodshot, streaks of red matching the flecks on her lips. The gun slung from her shoulder was forgotten. Sufan Noyoka's was not. He kept his hand on the weapon, the muzzle lifting to aim at Marek, falling as if by an effort of will, lifting again as if with a life of its own.

"No," said Dumarest.

"What?" Sufan turned, startled, his eyes a liquid darting. "What do you mean?"

"Don't hold your gun that way. There could be an accident and Marek is in the line of fire."

"He—"

"Annoys you. I know. And you must know that is exactly what he intends to do. He can't help it—but again, you know that."

"I do." Sufan lifted his hand from the gun and looked at it. The fingers trembled. "If we could do without him. The girl—"

"Can't lead us as he can. And with Jarv dead we still have to navigate the Cloud. She can help but only to a point. Control your anger."

"Yes, Earl, you're right, and you can see now why I needed you. At times like this tempers get frayed and no loyalty can be relied on. I don't trust Marek, he needs to be watched. If the whim takes him he will plunge us all into danger."

"Tell me of his past."

"I know little. He was a brilliant student and gained a high place in the Frenshi Institute. He married, had a child, and then something happened. Both died. Rumor hinted that he was responsible, a faulty judgment of some kind. After that he traveled for a time. You understand that I have no firsthand information."

"And?"

"We met. He was interested in Balhadorha. He could help. That's all."

A man tormented by guilt; it would account for his courting danger. A complex means of committing suicide, a psychological quirk—if Sufan was telling the truth. If he was, then Marek was more dangerous than a short-fused bomb.

Dumarest joined the man as he reached the opening. Beyond lay another chamber, long and narrow, an elongated bubble which ran to either side, each end marked with an opening. On the floor the tracery of thin black lines ended in a single complex pattern running evenly along the major axis.

"A dead end," said Marek. He looked at the blank wall facing them. "The end of the line."

"The treasure?"

"Lies beyond that wall, Earl. On a lower level, perhaps, but still beyond."

Dumarest looked upward. Lacking the other's talent, he could only guess, but he estimated that they must be either at the edge of the central spire or very close. The tracery of lines also offered a clue. The ending could be a line of demarcation.

"We must try one of the openings," he said. "Which? Left or right?"

For answer Marek dropped his hand to the gun slung over his shoulder, lifted it, cradled it, and clamped his finger on the trigger. Sound roared through the chamber as the muzzled vented a hail of bullets, slugs which struck to ricochet in whining, invisible death.

At the entrance Pacula cried out, threw herself before Embira, and hurled the girl to the ground. Sufan Noyoka, snarling, threw himself flat, his own gun lifting. Usan Labria slumped, a streak of red marring the line beneath her hair.

"Marek!" Dumarest lunged at the man, his hand gripping the barrel, lifting it as his stiffened palm chopped at the wrist. "Stop firing, you fool!"

"The wall—" Marek blinked at it as he rubbed his bruised arm. "I thought it would yield!"

A lie. The man hadn't thought, the action had stemmed from frustration and anger. A child kicking at an obstacle or a man seeking his own destruction. Dumarest tore the magazine from the weapon, threw both it and the gun aside, then ran to where Usan lay, eyes closed, blood staining the floor beneath her head.

"He killed her." Sufan Noyoka rose to his feet, his eyes blazing. "Earl—"

"She isn't dead." Dumarest lifted his canteen and poured water over the lax features. Carefully he examined the wound, the skin had been torn but the bone was unbroken. Beneath the impact of chemical vapors she stirred, opening her eyes, sitting upright with the help of his arm, wincing.

"Earl, what happened?"

"Marek tried to kill us all," snapped Sufan. "The fool must have known the bullets would ricochet. Pacula?"

"I'm all right." Gently she helped the girl to her feet. "Embira?"

"What happened? There was noise and then something threw me down. Earl?"

"Marek lost his head. It won't happen again."

Sufan said, "He tried to kill us. Had he turned and lifted his gun I would have shot him. He knew that, so tried a more subtle way."

"I made a mistake," said Marek. "If I had wanted to kill you, Sufan Noyoka, you would be dead now. But if you demand satisfaction? On Teralde the duel is common, I understand."

"There'll be no dueling," said Dumarest coldly. "And there will be no more stupidity." He glanced at the wall, the surface was unscarred. "You should have warned us, Marek, given us time to take cover."

"As I said, Earl, a mistake."

"Make another and it could be your last." Dumarest lifted the old woman to her feet. "Take care of Usan and guide us. Which way should we go? Left or right?"

Marek looked at the floor. The little pool of blood shed from Usan's wound lay at his feet like a crimson teardrop.

"The floor isn't level," he said. "Or the blood would not have run. We must follow the descent. To the right, Earl. The right."

Three hours later they looked at the treasure of Balhadorha.

The chambers had followed the path of a spiral, each slightly curved, all following a subtle gradient, the last ending in a room pierced with rounded openings. Beyond them lay a vast colonnade. Dumarest led the way across the smooth floor and halted at the far edge.

Beside him Sufan Noyoka sucked in his breath. Usan said uncertainly, "Is this, it, Earl? The treasure?"

"The treasure." Marek was positive. "There it is, my friends, the thing you have risked your lives to gain. The fabulous treasure of a fabled world." His laughter was thin, cynically bitter, devoid of genuine mirth. "So much for legend."

"But there's nothing," said Pacula. "Nothing!"

Nothing but an area wreathed with mist which stretched before them and to either side. A circular space ringed by the vast colonnade, the curved arms diminished by distance, arches and pillars taking on the appearance of a delicate filigree. Overhead light glowed from the surface of an inverted cone; the interior of the central spire. Dumarest stared up at it, his eyes blurred by the coils of rising mist, a thin vapor which turned in on itself, to fall, to rise again, to seeth in restless motion.

"Nothing," said Usan Labria. She sagged, leaning against a pillar, dwarfed by its immensity. "Nothing but dirt and mist. Earl, there has to be a mistake. There has to be!"

"We've been misled." Sufan Noyoka's voice betrayed his anger. "There should be—Marek, is this your idea of a jest?"

"I tried to warn you," said Marek. "But you refused to understand. What is treasure? It is and has to be something which men hold to be valuable. But even men have different concepts of value. The bone of a martyr to one could be a thing beyond price, to another nothing more than a scrap of useless tissue. A set of coordinates, to Earl, would be worth all he has and could hope to possess. Usan wants to be young. Pacula wants to find her child. And you, Sufan, what did you hope to find? Cash? The realization of a dream? A new discovery?"

Dumarest said, "And you, Marek? Peace?"

"Peace." For a moment he looked haggard, his face bearing his true age. "A word, Earl, but can you realize what it means? Can anyone? To be at rest, to be free of regret, never to be tormented with doubt, to be sure and never to wonder if only— Peace, Earl. Peace."

Dumarest said quietly, "The past is dead, Marek."

"Gone, but never dead, Earl. And I think you know it. Always it is with us in our memories. A glimpse of a face, the touch of a breeze, the scent of a flower, the echo of a song, and suddenly the past is with us. A thousand things, tiny triggers impossible to wholly avoid, and those gone rise to live again. To live. To accuse!"

"Marek!" Pacula moved forward to lay her hand on his arm. "Marek. Please!"

He stood a man transfigured, one grown suddenly old, his shoulders stooped, his face ravaged, stripped of the cynical mask. His hands were before him, slightly raised, the fingers clenched, the knuckles white with strain. A man exposed, vulnerable, and a little pathetic. More than a little easy to understand.

To die by his own hand would be too easy and never could he be sure that, even in death, he would find the peace he sought. It was better to tempt danger, to risk the destruction dealt by others and so, always, he invited punishment.

Watching him Pacula realized it and, realizing, understood how much they had in common. She, too, lived with guilt. Had she been a little more attentive, a little less easily pursuaded, Culpea would be alive now. Alive and grown and at her side. A girl of twelve, one at puberty, blossoming from child into woman and needing a mother's love. If only—

"Marek," she said again. "Please don't hurt yourself."

He stiffened a little, shoulders squaring, the mask falling over his face and eyes. Deliberately he unclenched his hands and looked at the fingers as he flexed them. A moment and he had become a stranger, but she had seen and recognized the real man and her hand did not fall from his arm.

Usan said, "Earl, my head. It aches like hell and I'm tired. To have come so far for so little. Nothing but dirt and mist." Her laughter was strained, artificial. "An old fool," she said. "That's what they called me. Well, maybe they were right after all. I'm old, certainly, and there is the evidence that I'm a fool." Her hand lifted to gesture at the open expanse, the mist. "We are all fools."

"No." Sufan Noyoka was insistent. "There has to be a mistake. The rumors must have some foundation. We must keep looking. Somewhere in the city we shall find it. The real treasure of Balhadorha. It has to be here."

"You are stubborn, Sufan." Marek dropped his hand to cover Pacula's, his fingers tightening as if he found a comfort in the warmth of her own. "I've solved the puzzle. What you see is the only treasure you will find. I swear it."

"You're mistaken! You have to be! I—"

"You're tired," said Dumarest sharply. The man's voice had risen to poise on the edge of hysteria. "We all are and

Usan's hurt. She needs to sleep. Later we can examine the area. There might be something in the mist."

"Yes." Sufan snatched at the suggestion like a starving dog at a bone. "Yes, Earl, that must be it. The mist, of course, it would hide the treasure. We must look for it."

"Later," said Dumarest. "First we sleep."

Chapter 15

Dumarest woke after two hours at the touch of Marek's hand. The man had stood the first watch—a precaution Dumarest had insisted on—and had seemed glad to do it. An opportunity to be alone, perhaps, though he and Pacula had spoken together before she had gone to rest.

"Earl?"

"I'm awake. Anything?"

"No, but Usan is restless and so is the girl. I heard her moaning." His voice held a note of concern. "To be blind in a place like this! Earl, without us she'd wander until she died!"

"You care?"

"Yes. A weakness, but I care. Somehow she has touched me and I—"

"Remember?" Dumarest's voice was soft. "Another girl, perhaps? Another woman. Who does she remind you of, Marek? Your wife?"

"You know?"

"A little. What happened?"

"Something I prefer not to remember, yet I cannot forget. My wife and daughter. She would have been a little younger than Embira. That surprises you?" His hand drifted toward his face. "Always I have looked young. A genetic trait, but that is not important. I was clever, proud of my skill, unable to consider the possibility I could ever be wrong. There was sickness, a mutated plague carried by a trader, and both fell victim. I knew exactly what had to be done. A selected strain of antibiotic, untested, but logically the answer. Something developed by the Cyclan."

Dumarest said flatly, "And?"

"I went to them and begged for a supply. They gave it at a price. My germ plasm for experimental uses—I would have given my life!"

129

And had given it, in a way; his seed used to breed, the genes manipulated so as to strengthen his trait, raw material used by the Cyclan in their quest for the perfect type.

"And the antibiotic failed?"

"It failed." Marek's voice was bitter. "Had I waited a few more days, a week at the most, all would have been well. A vaccine had been developed and—"

"You didn't know," said Dumarest. "And it wouldn't have helped. You did your best."

"I killed them, Earl. I went begging for the thing which took their life. The Cyclan warned me of the danger but I wouldn't listen. And what did they care? To them it was a test, no more. Had they lived I would have been in their debt and how could I have refused what they asked?"

By a simple rejection, but he wouldn't have thought of that. To him they would have given life and repayment would have been in small ways. Without knowing it he would have become an agent of the Cyclan.

Perhaps he was one? Dumarest studied the man's face and decided against it. His grief was too restrained, too deeply etched into his being. Too honest to blame others he had taken the fault on himself, but never could he forget those who had placed the instrument of death into his hands.

He said, "Get some sleep, now Marek."

"I'm not tired."

"Then rest, close your eyes and relax." He added, "Later Pacula and the girl could need you."

She was restless as Marek had said, twisting where she lay, her lips moving as if she cried out in nightmare. Gently he touched her, his hand caressing the golden mane of her hair, and, like a child, she turned toward him.

"Earl?"

"I'm here, Embira. Go back to sleep now. Relax and sleep. Sleep."

"Stay with me, darling. Stay . . ."

She had been barely awake and drifted into sleep as he watched. Usan was also restless but with more obvious cause. The wound on her scalp showed an ugly redness, inflammation spreading from the torn area. Beneath his touch Damarest felt a fevered heat.

Rising he walked to the opening of the chamber in which they had settled. Strands ran across it attached to canteens; if anything touched the ropes an alarm would be given. Turning he walked through the room and out on the colonnade.

The silence was complete.

It was something almost tangible as if sound had never been discovered. A heavy, brooding stillness in which the slight tap of the gun he carried against a pillar roared like thunder. There were no echoes, the sound dying as if muffled in cotton. Standing, he looked at the mist.

At the treasure of Balhadorha.

It was nothing, just mist rising above an open area, the vapor thick toward the center and shielding the ground. Its continuous movement caught and held his attention, plumes drifting to fall, to rise again as if touched by an unfelt wind or stirred by invisible forces. A swirling which, like the leaping flames of an open fire, gave birth to images of fantasy. A chelach, a krell, the face of a man long dead, a smiling woman, the twisting thrust of a naked blade.

Dumarest blinked and they were gone, but the mist remained, a fleecy cloud of bluish gray illuminated by the soaring height of the inverted cone. A kaleidoscope, devoid of color, replacing it with moving form and substance, whisps and tendrils forming patterns and hinting at familiar objects.

Had those who built the city worshiped here? Had they streamed from their chambers to stand in the colonnade, eyes toward the center, attention focused, adoring the mist? There were stranger objects of adoration. On Yulthan men knelt before a mass of meteoic iron chanting to the accompaniment of murmuring gongs. On Kaldarah women praised a mighty tree and wore bells which tinkled with delicate chimings as they danced.

One man's meat was another man's poison. One man's cross was another man's treasure.

Was Marek right? Was the mist all there was to be found in the city?

If so, what of his hopes of finding the location of Earth?

"Earl!" The cry was a scream cutting the air with the impact of edged steel. "Earl! For God's sake! No! No!"

Embira's voice carrying a raw terror. Dumarest jerked, turned, saw the edge of the colonnade fifty feet away, reached it at a run, the gun cradled in his arms. Sufan Noyoka glared at him, fighting with Marek's aid, to hold a struggling figure.

"Earl!" he panted. "Quickly! The girl's gone mad!"

She was like a thing possessed, her body arching, muscles taut beneath the skin, a thin rill of spittle running from her mouth. Her blind eyes were wide, starting, her face disfigured with pain.

"Embira!" Dumarest reached her, touched her face, her throat. There was no time for drugs. Already the tension of her muscles threatened to snap bone and tear ligaments. His fingers found the carotids, pressed, cutting off the blood supply to the brain. Within seconds she slumped, unconscious, relaxing as she fell. "What happened?"

"I don't know." Sufan Noyoka dabbed at his face. The girl's fingernails had drawn deep furrows over his cheek. "I'd woken and was getting food when suddenly she screamed and went mad."

"Not mad." Pacula eased the girl's limbs and drew hair from her face and eyes. "She must have had an attack of some kind. I was getting water from one of the canteens when I heard her cry out. The rest you know." Pausing, she said bleakly. "Did you have to hurt her?"

"I didn't."

"But the way you gripped! There are bruises on her throat!"

"She will wake feeling no worse than if she had fainted." Dumarest looked at Cognez. "Marek?"

"I must have been dosing. I woke when she screamed. Sufan had hold of her." He added meaningfully, "Maybe that's why she screamed."

"A lie! It happened as I said!" Sufan Noyoka's voice grew ugly. "Is this another of your attempts at humor, Marek? If it is I warn you now. My Patience is exhausted. Try me further and I will—"

"Kill me?" Marek spread his arms in invitation. "Then do it now. Do it—and then wonder how you are to escape this maze. Unless the girl recovers who else can guide you? And who will help to carry your treasure?" His laughter held a naked scorn. "The treasure. Sufan, you don't have to kill me. I give you my share willingly."

"That's enough!" snapped Dumarest. He stood, watching the others. "Why did you wake, Sufan?"

"Why?" The man blinked, baffled by the question. "Because I had rested long enough, I suppose."

"Nothing woke you? No sound?"

"No, but if there had been anything surely you would have heard it. You were on watch, remember?"

"Pacula, were the canteens disturbed?"

"No, and I heard nothing. Like Sufan I woke because I had slept long enough."

"It's five hours since I woke you Earl," said Marek quietly. "You should have called me to take my turn on watch."

"Five hours?" Dumarest said. "Pacula, have sedatives ready, Embira may need them when she recovers. Sufan, if you want food you'd better get it ready. Some for the others also."

"And you, Earl?"

"I'm not hungry." It was true, he felt both fed and rested and had no thirst. Even the dull ache of the bruised flesh of his back had vanished.

As Sufan broke food from the packs, crumbling concentrates into water which he placed over a heating element and breaking more from a slab, Pacula said, "What caused it, Earl?"

"Embira?"

"Yes." She glanced at the limp figure. "A fit? A seizure of some kind? But what triggered it? If I thought Sufan was responsible I'd kill him."

A cold statement of fact, the more chilling because spoken without emotion.

"He wasn't," said Dumarest. "She must have caught his face by accident. Perhaps she'd lowered her guard. She was afraid of something lying within the city. I told her to blank it out if she could, but she was asleep and maybe couldn't maintain her defenses." He glanced at the girl as she stirred. "Have those sedatives ready, Pacula. She might need them."

"You could do her more good than drugs, Earl. She needs you."

"Perhaps—but so does Usan."

She lay like a broken doll, her breathing ragged, her face flushed with an unhealthy tinge. As Dumarest touched her she stirred, her eyes opening, the corners crusted with dried pus, her lips spotted with dried saliva. Incredibly she smiled.

"Earl! I was dreaming—how did you know?"

"Know what?"

"That I'd want you beside me when I woke." Her voice was husky. "A drink?"

She gulped the water he fetched her, leaning hard against his supporting arm. With a damp cloth he laved her face and cleared her eyes. The stench of her breath signaled inner dissolution. Aware of it she turned her face.

"Here." He handed her the open locket. "You'd better take something."

"For the pain?" Her smile was a travesty of humor. "I'm getting used to it, Earl. You don't have to worry about me." Her eyes moved, settled on where Pacula knelt beside Embira. "What happened to the girl?"

"A fit, maybe. She screamed and went into convulsions."

Without comment she rose and climbed to her feet, to stand swaying for a moment, gaining strength with a visible effort. Beads of sweat stood on the sunken cheeks and droplets of blood showed beneath the teeth biting her lower lip.

"You're ill, Usan. You should rest."

"I'm dying, Earl, and we both know it. When the drugs are gone I'll be in hell and they won't last much longer. Maybe you should do me a favor. A bullet, your knife—you know how to do it."

"Kill you, Usan? No."

"Why not? Would you deny me that mercy?" Her voice was hard. "Would you?"

"If it was necessary, no." His voice was equally hard. "But you've too much courage to plead for death. What's happened to your spirit? The determination to survive? Have you forgotten that young and lovely body you hope to gain?"

"A dream, Earl and one that's fading. If I leave this place it will be only because you carry me. And then there is the Cloud and the journey to Pane and how will I pay the surgeons? With mist?"

"There could be something."

"Under the mist? Perhaps." Her fingers fumbled at the locket and she lifted pills to her mouth. "Water, Earl?" She drank and waited for the drugs to take effect. It had been a heavy dose, too heavy for safety, but what did that matter now? "Sufan, when do we search?"

He looked up from where he sat, a container in his hand, a spoon lifted halfway toward his mouth.

"Later, Usan, when we have eaten. Then I—"

"Not you, Sufan. Me. I must be the first. You'll not deny me that?"

Dumarest said, "It could be dangerous."

"If so the more reason I should go first. What have I to lose? Earl, arrange it." Then, as he hesitated, she added quietly, "Please, Earl. At least let me be sure there is hope."

The danger lay in the unknown. The mist thickened toward the center of the area, forming an almost solid wall of writhing fog, and once within it orientation would be lost and the woman could wander until she dropped. The ground, too, could be treacherous. At the outer edge it was firm, but deeper in the mist there could be soft patches, holes, anything. And, if treasure did lie in heaps, it alone could provide hazards.

All this Dumarest explained as they stood on the floor of the wide colonnade.

"I know, Earl." Usan was impatient. "I know."

"Go in, find out what you can and return. This will guide you." Dumarest lifted the coil he held, a thin rope he'd made of plaited strands taken from a thicker coil. "I'll tie it around your waist. When you want to return take up the slack and follow the line. You understand?"

"Yes." She sagged a little, then straightened, her breathing harsh. "But hurry, Earl. Hurry!"

The line attached she stepped from the colonnade and headed toward the mist. The line snaked from where it lay in a coil on the floor, the other end fastened to Dumarest's wrist.

Marek said, "A woman of courage, Earl, but as she said, what has she to lose? How long will you allow her to search?"

"Not long."

"Earl!" Sufan frowned as Dumarest looked toward him. "If anything happens to her, what then?"

"It hasn't yet."

"But if it does? She's old and ill and near collapse. She could die out there, but if she does we must continue to search. I insist on that."

Marek said, "She's gone."

The mist had closed about her, streamers and coils writhing, drifting, reforming as they watched. Dumarest felt a tug at his wrist and looked at the line. It was extended, taut as it vanished into the mist. Gently he tugged at it, again, the cord dipping to lie on the ground.

"How long will you give her?" said Marek. "An hour?"

"More," said Sufan. "We must give her a chance to search. The more we learn the better, and if—" He broke off, but there was no need of words. If danger lay within the mist and she should fall victim to it her death would at least warn the others.

All they could do now was to wait.

Pacula came to join them. She said, "How long are you going to leave her out there? It's been hours."

Hours? Dumarest said, "Get back to Embira."

"She's resting. Asleep. The sedatives—"

"Get back to her!"

Dumarest looked at the line. It lay thin and straight without movement of any kind. If Usan had found something and was examining it the line would present that appearance. If she was moving a little from side to side or returning it would be the same. But too much time had passed. She could have fallen to be lying unconscious or dead.

Marek said, "Hours? Earl, that doesn't make sense. But Usan—you'd better bring her back."

Dumarest was already at work. Quickly he drew in the line, feeling no resistance, continuing to pull it back until the end came into sight.

"She's gone!" Sufan's voice was high, incredulous. "Earl! She's vanished!"

"She untied the line." Marek stooped, lifted it in his hands. "See? No sign of a break. Maybe she saw something she couldn't reach and undid the knot. Now she's lost." He stared at the mist, the vast, shrouded area. "Lost," he said again. "Earl, what happens now?"

Dumarest said, "I'm going to find her."

Chapter 16

The line had been extended and was firm about his waist. The others were watching, aside from Embira who was still asleep, but Dumarest didn't turn to look at them. Marek held the line and a loop was attached to a pillar. Sulfan had been full of instructions, heard and ignored. Dumarest would operate in his own way.

Beneath his feet the ground held a gentle slope, checked by a glance at the colonnade to one side. A saucer like depression, not a hemisphere or the ground would have held a sharper gradient. A shallow bowl then, why hadn't he noticed it before?

Around him the mist began to thicken.

It held a trace of pungency, an odor not unpleasant, slightly reminiscent of the fur of a cat, the tang of spice. It filled his nostrils as he breathed and stung his eyes a little, a discomfort which passed as soon as noticed. He had expected to be blinded by the mist but always, as he walked, it seemed to open before him. An area of visibility a few yards in diameter. The ground was smoothly even, yielding like a firm sponge beneath his boots, which left no trace of their passage.

"Usan!" The mist flattened his call. "Usan!"

She could be anywhere and finding her would be a matter of luck. Already he had lost all sense of direction, only the line offering a guide.

"Usan!"

A woman, old, sick, dying, but with greater courage than most. Kalin had been like that. Kalin, who had gained what Usan most desired, a new and healthy body, living as a host in another's shape. Using the secret he carried, the one given to her by her husband before he died, passing it on in turn.

Kalin—could he ever forget her?

And then, incredibly, she was before him.

"Earl! My darling! My lover—I have waited so long!"

She came from the mist, tall, her hair a scarlet flame, eyes wide, lips parted, hands lifted to grasp his shoulders. Against his chest he could feel the pressure of her body, her sensual heat.

"Earl, my darling! My darling!"

He felt the touch of her lips, her hands, the swell of breasts and hips, the long, lovely curve of her thighs. All as he remembered—but Kalin was dead. Kalin, the real Kalin—not the beautiful shell she had worn.

"Come with me, Earl." She took his hand and led him to a room bright with sparkling color. A wide bed rested on a soft carpet, flowers filled vases of delicate crystal, perfume hung on the summer air. From beyond the open window came the sound of birds. "Rest, my darling, and talk to me. But first— Her kiss was warm with promise, her flesh inviting to his touch. "Again, my darling. Again!"

Dumarest drew a long, shuddering breath. He was a man and within him was sensual yearning, little desires and hopes building into fantastic imagery, the biological drives inherent in any normal human. To love and be loved, to need and be needed, to have and to hold. And yet—

"Is something wrong, Earl?" The woman looked at him, her eyes filled with stars. "Earl! Don't you remember me?"

Too well and in too great a detail. The line of her chin, the tilt of her head, the little quirk at the corners of her lips. He studied them again, his eyes dropping to the gown she wore, short, cut low, shimmering emerald belted with a band of scarlet the color of her hair. All real as the room was real, the flowers. He picked one, the crushed bloom falling from his hand.

"Earl?"

"No," he said. "No."

And was again surrounded by mist.

It looked as before, a swirling, bluish gray fog, smoke in constant motion as if with a life of its own. The smoke of fires remembered from earlier days when as a boy he had crouched over smoldering embers cooking the game fallen to his sling. A lesson learned then never to be forgotten. Eat or die. Kill or starve. Survive or perish. Childhood had not been a happy time.

But Earth was his home. Earth!

The mist parted and he stood on a meadow. The softness

of lush grass was beneath his feet and trees soared in ancient
grace to one side. A moment and he was among them to
walk among the boles of a natural cathedral. The trunks were
rough to his touch, the leaf he thrust into his mouth succulent
with juices, the little wad of masticated fiber falling to the
soft, rich soil.

The trees yielded to a clearing slashed by a stream fringed
with willows, the tinkle of water over stone a somnolent
music in the warm, scented air. In the azure sky hung the
pale orb of the Moon, a silver ghost blotched with familiar
markings.

Home. He was home!

Not the one remembered from boyhood, the bleak area of
ravaged stone and arid soil, the haunts of small and vicious
beasts, of poverty and savage men, but the one he had always
been convined must lie over the horizon. Earth as it had
been. Earth as it should be. Warm and gentle and filled with
enchantment.

A paradise.

The only one there ever was or ever could be.

"You like it?" A man rose from where he had been sitting
at the edge of the stream. His face was shadowed by the cowl
of his brown, homespun robe, his hands thrust into its sleeves.
His voice held the deep resonance of a bell.

"You?"

"A friend. An ear to listen and a mouth to talk. Each man
needs a friend, Earl. Someone to understand."

A need supplied as soon as felt. Dumarest said, "This is
Earth? There can be no mistake?"

"This is Earth, Earl. How can you doubt? Your home, the
only world on which you can feel whole. Can you understand
why? Every cell of your body was fashioned and shaped by
this place. It is the only planet on which you can feel wholly
in tune, to which you can ever really belong. Look around
you. Everything you see is a part of you; the grass, the trees,
the creatures which walk and swim and fly. The water, the
sunlight, the glow of the Moon. Only here can you ever find
true contentment, Earl. Only on Earth can you ever find happiness."

And he was happy with a pleasure he had never before
known or had even dreamed could exist. An intoxication of
supreme bliss which caused him to stoop, to fill his hands
with dirt, to lift them and let it rain before his eyes.

Earth!

His home now and for always.

The days would shorten and winter come with snow and crisp winds. There would be growth and harvest and the regular pattern of life to which he would respond. And there would be others, of that he was certain. Men and women to offer him a welcome. A wife, children, sons to teach and daughters to cherish. An end to loneliness.

"Earl!"

He frowned at the sound of his name. Who could be calling him?"

"Earl. I need you. Please help me. Earl!" A woman's voice holding pain and terror, things which had no place in this ideal. It came again, louder, "For God's sake where are you? Answer me, Earl. I need you. Earl. Earl!"

A flash of movement. Derai? But the hair was gold, not silver, and the eyes were blind.

"Embira!"

She came to him from the mist, hands lifted, groping, her face dewed with sweat which carried the scent of her fear. A woman alone, blind, and afraid, walking into the unknown. The line firmly knotted around her waist trailed behind her. His own, Dumarest noticed, was gone. When had he freed himself from its restraint?

"Earl?" Her hands caught his own, the fingers closing with an iron grip. "Thank God I've found you! We waited so long and your line was cut and—Earl! Don't leave me!"

"I won't, Embira."

"It hurts," she said dully. "The pain, the hunger and fear. I'm so afraid. Take me back, Earl. Take me back."

Freeing his hands, he turned her, clamping his left arm around her shoulders, catching up the line with his right. He pulled, drawing in the slack and, when it was taut, jerked three times. An answering jerk and the line tightened, dragging at the girl's waist.

Marek was at the far end, Pacula and Sufan at his side. As Dumarest reached the edge of the colonnade and guided the girl into Pacula's waiting arms, Marek said, "So she found you. Thank God for that. I'd about given up hope. When we pulled in your line and found it cut—"

Sufan interrupted, his voice impatient. "What did you find, Earl? What is the treasure of Balhadorha?"

Dumarest answered in one word. "Death."

The food and water were getting low but Dumarest had no need of them and neither did the girl. The mist had taken care of them both, removing toxins, nourishing tissue, maintaining life in its own fashion. But while Dumarest had suffered no apparent ill effects the girl had collapsed. She lay on the floor of the far side of the chamber, her face drawn, stamped with signs of anguish despite the drugs which dulled her senses.

"She volunteered," said Marek quietly. "When you didn't return and we found your line cut she insisted on going after you. She said that she alone could find you."

"She was right."

"As events proved, Earl. Her talent, of course, it makes her something other than normal. But you were in the mist for a long time. Long enough for Sufan to make a circuit of the area."

"I found nothing." The man came forward, eyes darting. "And you, Earl?"

"I told you."

"Death—what answer is that? Did you find anything beneath the mist? Artifacts? Gems? Anything at all?"

"I found everything the legends promised. Wealth beyond imagination, pleasure unexpected, the answers to all questions, the solution to all problems. It's all there in the mist." Dumarest stared toward it, the swirling vapors edged by the openings set in the wall of the chamber. "The rumors didn't lie. Everything you could hope for is there, but at a price."

"Death," said Pacula, and shivered. "Earl, what is it?"

"A symbiote."

"Alive?" Marek was incredulous. "After so long?"

"Time is different within the mist. An hour becomes a minute. Perhaps the colonnade has something to do with it, or the city. It isn't important. But that mist is alive. It takes something, a little blood, some bone marrow, the aura of emotion, perhaps, but feeding, it gives. Each thought and wish becomes real. The host is maintained in a world of illusion. One so apparently real that it is impossible to escape."

"But you escaped, Earl."

"With Embira's help, Pacula. If she hadn't come looking for me I would be there still."

"And you long to return." She looked at him with sudden understanding. "Earl—"

"I must try it," said Sufan. "I must experience it for myself. If I am tied to a line I should be safe."

"You would free yourself from the line," said Dumarest. "Nothing would stop you. If you were locked in steel it might be possible, but we have no metal straps and chain. If you go in you'll stay in."

"Maybe it's worth it." Marek looked at the mist, his eyes thoughtful. "What more can life offer than total satisfaction? If what you say is true, Earl, then here we have found happiness."

"And Embira?"

"What of her?"

"She can't share that happiness, Marek. Do you want to leave her here, alone, blind, terrified? She needs us. We must take her back to the ship. And we need you to help guide us through the Cloud."

"Need," said Marek bitterly. "What is another's need to me?" But he began collecting the packs, the weapons and supplies.

Pacula said, "Earl! What of Usan Labria?"

"We leave her."

"Usan? But—"

She was at the heart of the mist, lying on the softly firm ground, tended by the alien organism in return for what she could give. The very substance of her body, perhaps, disintegrating after death to culminate the bargain. But while alive, she was freed of pain and locked in a world of fantasy. Perhaps she ran light-footed over emerald sward or acted the queen in some luxurious palace. Around her would be attentive lovers and, in mirrors, she would relish the sight of her lovely young body. Happiness would be hers—what more could life offer?

"We have no choice," said Dumarest. "We can't find her, and even if we could, to rescue her would be cruel. She'd be dead before we left the Cloud and without money what can she hope for? Now she is happy." He said again, harshly. "We leave her."

Leave! To turn his back on paradise!

He felt a touch on his arm and looked down to see Pacula's hand. Her eyes, inches below his own, were soft with concern.

"You don't want to go, do you, Earl? You're doing this for Embira. If you were alone would you stay? Would you go back into the mist?"

To Kalin and others he had known. To the planet of his birth and the incredible pleasure which had filled him, the content and utter satisfaction.

He said unsteadily, "If I went again into the mist I'd never return. Now, for God's sake, woman, let's be on our way!"

As she went to lift the girl to her feet Dumarest looked at the others. Both were ready. Sufan Noyoka stepped to the near edge of the colonnade, breathing deeply, taking a final look at the treasure he had spent his life to find.

Dumarest had expected him to argue, instead he accepted the departure, his face calm as he led the way from the chamber.

The women followed him, Pacula supporting the girl.

"So it's over, Earl." Marek shrugged and adjusted pack and gun. "For now, at least, but Sufan will be back. I'm certain of it. Nothing will keep him away and his friends will help him."

"Has he any left?"

"I use the word in its general sense, Earl. The Cyclan is the friend of no man, but they will be interested in what he has to tell them. This place could be put to use and they will be happy to learn of it—if a cyber can ever be happy. They will stake him on a second expedition."

To investigate the mist. To take samples, to test, perhaps to breed fresh organisms. To create new centers and so gain another weapon in their war to dominate all Mankind. A bribe or a gift to those who were loyal. The old and sick and miserable given paradise. The rich and jaded offered a supreme thrill. Once established each center would dominate a world.

Dumarest said bleakly, "Will the Cyclan listen to him?"

"Why not? They are old associates." Marek was bitter. "Didn't he tell you? That's where we first met, in the laboratory which gave me the thing to kill my wife and child. He was asking advice or something, but he was there."

As associate of his enemy—no wonder he had been followed to Chamelard and beyond. The vessel chasing them must have been lost in the Cloud, but there would be others, more cybers waiting to plot his movements, waiting where they would know he would be.

"Earl?"

"Nothing," said Dumarest. "Let's get after the others."

Chapter 17

They walked through silent chambers, following the upward path of the spiral, reaching the one stained with a pool of dried blood. Marek had taken the lead and guided them through the brooding maze back to where a dead man lay on a bed of dust. Through the circular openings streamed the light of the yellow and crimson suns, warm swaths which touched the sunken cheeks and rictus of the smile.

Captain Cleeve Inchelan seemed amused.

"His raft," said Marek. "If we could only find his raft."

If there was one at all. If the structure was undamaged and the power intact—a small hope after so long.

To Pacula, Dumarest said, "How is the girl?"

She sat with her back against a wall, her face dull, her hands lying listlessly in her lap. Not once had she spoken during the journey, walking like a person in a daze, one semi-stunned or drugged. But the sedatives she had been given would have lost their effect by now.

Touching her cheek, Dumarest said gently, "Embira?"

"She's in shock," said Pacula. "That damned mist!"

The impact of the alien organism on her mind. Her talent strained by its aura, her ego withdrawing to a place of imagined safety. Looking at her Dumarest could appreciate what she had done. To walk into the glare of burning magnesium, eyes forced open, tormented yet searching for the flicker of a candle which had been himself. Conscious of the hunger of the thing, the danger.

"Embira?" His hand stroked her cheek. "Embira, talk to me."

"Earl?" Her voice was a whisper. "Earl?"

"You're getting through," said Pacula. "Try again." Her own hand gripped the girl's. "You're safe now, Embira. Safe."

"My head—it hurts. I can't—Earl!"

She clung to him like a child.

Sufan Noyoka said, "Can she guide us? Lead us through the chambers back to the door? Ask her, Earl. Ask her!"

"If she can't we're stuck," said Marek. "With luck I could find the door, but how to pass through it?" Looking at the dead man he added bleakly, "It might be that the captain will have company soon."

"Ask her!" snapped Sufan again. "Make her guide us!"

"She can't be forced." Dumarest rose, the girl's hands falling to lie again in her lap. "It will take time before she recovers, if she ever can within the city. We'll have to find another way out."

"How? The wall can't be climbed."

"From the outside, no," Dumarest admitted. "But from the inside? We'll have to find out. Marek!"

He led the man to one of the openings and together they climbed to the lower edge. It was set high on the curve of the chamber and, thrusting his head and shoulders far out, Dumarest turned to study the slope above. If the material was the same as that of the outer wall they had no chance, but if it was like that of the smaller chambers there was hope.

"Pass me a gun, Marek, and hold me firm."

Dumarest leaned back, his legs held by the other man, lifting the gun and aware of the danger inherent in the recoil. Aiming he fired, a long blast which left a scarred gash, shallow but deep enough to offer a precarious hold. Lifting the muzzle he fired again, again, blasting a ladder in the smooth surface.

As he ducked back through the opening Marek said, "Can we climb it?"

"Yes. I'll go first and drop a rope. We can pull the women up behind us."

"And after?"

"We'll see."

The roof was long, rounded, curved like the back of a whale. It ended at one of the mounds, a curved rainbow of shimmering, refracted light, which swept up and to either side.

Marek said, "Earl, the gun?" He grunted when the roar of the weapon died, leaving the surface unscarred. "Well, we were lucky once. What now?"

"We climb." Dumarest narrowed his eyes as he studied the

barrier. They were high against the curve, another dozen feet and they would be able to crawl, fifteen and they would be relatively safe. How to gain those fifteen feet?

"Pacula, lift your skirt up around your waist and tie it. Bare your legs and arms, those of the girl also. Marek, don't move!" Light flashed from the knife he lifted from his boot. With the edge he roughed the clothing the man wore, doing the same to Sufan, ending him himself. "It'll give extra traction," he explained, sheathing the blade. "Remember to lie flat and press hard against the surface. Use your flattened hands, a cheek, the insides of your legs."

Dumarest set the example, leaning to face the slope, straddling his legs as Marek climbed to his shoulders. Sufan followed, then Pacula. She inched forward, providing an anchor for Sufan, the two of them drawing up Marek to lie beside them.

"Embira." Dumarest fastened her to the rope and explained what had to be done. "You can manage?"

"If you're with me, Earl."

"I'll be with you." He guided her to the slope. "Up now."

He lifted her, his hands firm around her waist, moving to her thighs, her knees. His palms made cups to support her feet, the extension of his arms holding her high. With the others she would lie flat, providing an anchor to take his weight.

A procedure repeated as, like flies, they crawled over the mounds to the wall.

It rose ten feet against the sky, featureless, a blank expanse which ran to either side on its long circle about the city. Without hope Dumarest blasted it with a hail of bullets, the roar of the gun muted in the brooding stillness of the air.

"Now what?" Marek shook his head. "We could reach the summit but what will it gain us? There's a hundred-foot drop the other side."

"We have a rope."

"True, but how to hold it? There's nothing to tie it to, Earl. One could let down the others but how can he escape?"

Dumarest said, "Empty your packs. Drop the canteens and guns, all the weight you can. Now, you first, Pacula. Free the rope when you land."

"Embira?"

"Will follow, but she will need you to guide her. Now hurry, woman! Move!"

Quick action to save the need of thought, the realization of what would happen if she should fall. With the rope firmly knotted Dumarest took the slack, a loop around his waist, watching as Pacula climbed on Marek's shoulders. Turning to look at him she said, "Earl! What—"

She cried out as she slipped on the yielding surface, the rope streaming through Dumarest's hands, checking as he strained against it, slipping smoothly and easily through his hands. It slowed as he tightened his grip to lower the woman gently through the last stage of descent.

A moment, then a jerk and Dumarest drew back the rope.

"Embira!"

Sufan Noyoka followed leaving Marek and Dumarest alone.

"Your turn, Earl."

"Yours." Dumarest kicked at the empty packs. "Take those with you. Fill them with dirt and stone, anything which has weight. Tie them to the rope."

"I'm lighter than you are, Earl."

"Which is why you're going first. You may not be able to take my weight."

"The Knave of Swords," murmured Marek. "I was a fool. Not the Knave but the Lord. Without you—" He broke off then said flatly. "Earl, you realize you're trusting me with your life?"

There had been no choice—only he possessed the bulk to take the strain of the rope, the knowledge of what to do. Alone Dumarest checked the weight of the discarded equipment. The guns, the ammunition, the canteens, now almost empty, the food and other supplies. It wasn't enough. Without friction it could never hold his weight, and unless he had enough to anchor the rope, death was inevitable.

Death or the mist. A return to the heart of the city if he could make it. Injury and the torment of thirst if he could not.

Had the captain died trying vainly to reach paradise?

A tug and he hauled up the rope. It held only half the packs, each heavy with dirt. A second haul and he had enough. Dumarest lashed the packs, the guns and other things together, fastened them to the end of the rope, wrapped more around his waist. The loose end he threw over the wall, and without hesitation, followed it.

Timus Omilcar came running as Dumarest landed. The engineer was panting, sweat dewing his face. His voice boomed through the air as he came to a halt before the little group standing before the wall.

"You're back! Thank God for that! I was about to give up hope when I heard the gunfire. What happened? Where is the treasure?"

"There is no treasure," said Marek. "None we could carry and not what you hoped for."

"None? Nothing at all?" Timus searched them with his eyes. "Where's Usan?"

"We left her. We had no choice." Pacula added bleakly, "But she, at least, got what she came to find. The only one of us who did."

"No," said Dumarest. "Not the only one. You've been lucky, too."

"Lucky? How?"

"You came for money in order to search for your daughter. Haven't you realized yet that she stands at your side?"

"Culpea? No! Where—" She turned to stare at the girl. "Embira? Impossible!"

"Is it?" Dumarest stepped closer. Sufan Noyoka, he noticed, had backed a little, one hand fumbling at his wrist. "Think about it. Who was close when you lost her? You told me that Sufan Noyoka was in the area. Did you search his raft?"

"No. Of course not. He didn't—he wouldn't—Earl, she's too old!"

"Slow-time," he said. "Under it she would have aged a month in a day. Look at her arms. The elbows are scarred with inserts used for intravenous feeding. And remember how you felt when you first saw her, how you were drawn to her." And then, as still she stared her disbelief, "Look in a mirror, woman! Study her bones! You could have been sisters, you said, but the relationship is closer than that. She is your daughter."

"This is stupidity!" Sufan Noyoka's voice was brittle with anger. "Why are you talking like this, Earl? What is in your mind? What are you trying to do?"

"You deny it?"

"Certainly I deny it. Don't listen to him, Pacula. You have known me for years. Are you going to take the word of an adventurer against that of an old friend?"

She said uncertainly, "I don't know. I—how can I be sure?"

"You can be sure," said Dumarest. "There are tests which will prove it. We can do them in the ship. Sufan knows how to conduct them. He has biological knowledge and can settle the matter one way or the other."

"You're mad! Insane! Why should you think I have such skill?"

"Didn't the Cyclan teach you? Isn't that why you attended their laboratory? Why else did you visit them? Don't trouble to deny it, Marek saw you. You met there. Well?"

"I wanted advice. It had to do with Balhadorha. Earl, I warn you. Keep silent or—"

"You'll kill me as you did Jarv Nonach?" Dumarest shrugged. "You had to kill him, of course. He intended to leave and you couldn't allow that. Even less could you allow him the chance of being able to return. He could have charted a course and robbed you of your discovery and so he had to die. It was simple, a poison in his pomander, and how could you be blamed? And now that you know what lies in the city how many others do you intend to kill? Pacula? She isn't necessary. Marek? Perhaps, after he has helped to guide you. The engineer later—they come cheap. The only one you really need is Embira." Pausing, Dumarest added bitterly, "The girl you stole and had changed in the laboratories of the Schell-Peng. Blinded and trained, taught under slow-time, artificially aged, robbed of her childhood—and you call yourself an old friend!"

"You did that!" Pacula's face was that of a savage beast. "Sufan, you filth!"

"He's lying! Don't you understand? He's lying! Why should I do a thing like that?"

For answer Dumarest gestured at the city.

"For this. The dream of a lifetime, you said, and I believe you. As I believe those who called you mad. A madness which stopped at nothing. You needed the girl because of her genetic trait, one inherited from her father. He could see in the dark, you said, Pacula, but what more? Would you have known? Would he? But Sufan guessed and the Cyclan confirmed it. They told him what must be done if he hoped to fashion her into an instrument with which to navigate the Hichen Cloud. Eight years ago. Marek, when did you meet? Eight years ago? Nine?"

"About nine, Earl. Yes."

"And the land you went to examine, Sufan's land. A trap into which you fell, Pacula. He had the child drugged and hidden in his raft. Later he took her to Chamelard. If you doubt me the tests will decide."

Sufan Noyoka said, "That will be enough." His hand rose from his sleeve, metal glinting in the light. A laser, small but powerful enough to burn and kill. "A mistake, Earl. I was careless. I should have left you behind on Chamelard."

After he had won possession of the girl—but he could have had another reason and Dumarest suspected that he had. One which had determined his choice of action.

Pacula said, "Sufan, are you saying—"

"But of course, my dear. Earl is shrewd and has guessed the truth, but why be so upset? What is a single child worth against what we have found? And she is here, handicapped a little, perhaps, but with a unique talent."

He stepped back as she lunged toward him, hands extended, fingers reaching for his eyes. The laser blurred as he lashed out with its weight, the impact of metal against her temple loud in the heavy air. It lifted as she fell to lie twitching on the dirt.

"Move, Earl, and I fire. Not to kill, naturally, but you could do little with crippled legs. In fact it would be a sensible precaution. The knees, I think, and the elbows." The laser leveled in his hand.

Marek said, "No! Sufan, you can't!"

"You hope to stop me?" The weapon swung in Sufan's hand. "I need you, Marek, but can make do without you. You too, Timus. Stand back the pair of you. And think of the treasure—what is one man's life worth against what the city contains? I promised you wealth, and you shall have it, more than you can imagine. The Cyclan can be generous when it suits their aims. And now—no!"

Too late he realized his mistake, the lapse of attention which was all Dumarest needed. His hand dropped to his boot, lifted with the knife, steel hurtling as Sufan shouted, the blade turning as he fired, one shot which seared the tunic at Dumarest's shoulder.

Then he was down, blood streaming from his eye, staining his face, the dirt, the hilt of the knife buried in the socket and penetrating the brain.

"Earl!"

"I'm all right." Dumarest felt his shoulder, his fingers red when he lifted them from the shallow wound. "See to Pacula."

She rose as Marek reached her, her temple marred by an ugly bruise, her hands reaching toward the girl.

"Culpea! My child!"

"She'll be all right," said Marek. "We'll see to that, Pacula. If you will let me?"

The way of life, need meeting need, each recognizing the emptiness of the other, each ready to fill it, both to take care of the girl.

With time she would be herself again and more. New eyes could be grown from cell tissue to replace those deliberately blinded by the Schell-Peng in order to concentrate her mind on her talent.

"Earl?" Timus Omilcar looked at the dead man, the gleaming bulk of the city. "I suppose there's nothing more we can do here?"

"Nothing. Get back to the ship now. We leave as soon as the girl has rested."

Up and back through the Cloud, the ship sold and the money divided. Timus to go his own way, the others to return to Teralde, perhaps, the security of land and family, himself to move on.

Stooping, Dumarest jerked free his knife. Sufan Noyoka was dead and with him had died the immediate danger of the Cyclan. Had he known the value of the stranger he had carried? Dumarest thought it possible, but he could never have realized his true worth. More even than the fabled treasures of Balhadorha.

He looked for the last time at the city. It lay like a gem in the cupped palm of the hills, a cathedral or a tomb? Had those who built it lived to worship the mist? Had they, finally, succumbed to its attraction? Or had it been nothing more than an elaborate prison?

A housing for paradise?

Dumarest turned and headed toward the ship. The city held nothing but illusion, and Earth, the real Earth, had yet to be found.

Presenting JOHN NORMAN in DAW editions . . .

☐ **TRIBESMEN OF GOR.** The tenth novel of Tarl Cabot takes him face to face with the Others' most dangerous plot— in the vast Tahari desert with its warring tribes, its bandit queen, and its treachery. (#UW1223—$1.50)

☐ **HUNTERS OF GOR.** The saga of Tarl Cabot on Earth's orbital counterpart reaches a climax as Tarl seeks his lost Talena among the outlaws and panther women of the wilderness. (#UW1102—$1.50)

☐ **MARAUDERS OF GOR.** The ninth novel of Tarl Cabot's adventures takes him to the northland of transplanted Vikings and into direct confrontation with the enemies of two worlds. (#UW1160—$1.50)

☐ **TIME SLAVE.** The creator of Gor brings back the days of the caveman in a vivid lusty new novel of time travel and human destiny. (#UW1204—$1.50)

☐ **IMAGINATIVE SEX.** A study of the sexuality of male and female which leads to a new revelation of sensual liberation. Fifty-three imaginative situations are outlined, some of which are science-fictional in nature.
(#UJ1146—$1.95)

DAW BOOKS are represented by the publishers of Signet and Mentor Books, THE NEW AMERICAN LIBRARY, INC.

THE NEW AMERICAN LIBRARY, INC.,
P.O. Box 999, Bergenfield, New Jersey 07621

Please send me the DAW BOOKS I have checked above. I am enclosing $_____(check or money order—no currency or C.O.D.'s). Please include the list price plus 25¢ a copy to cover mailing costs.

Name_____

Address_____

City_____ State_____ Zip Code_____
Please allow at least 3 weeks for delivery